With one last look in the mirror, Piper grabbed the clutch and opened the door.

Right to Caleb Martin.

They both took a step back. Both sized each other up in the silence that followed. He wore light blue pants and a white shirt. It accentuated the brown of his skin, the broadness of his shoulders, the dark black of his hair. He'd shaved since they'd last seen one another, so the sharp angles of his face were even more striking than they'd been that afternoon. Or perhaps that was because he no longer wore sunglasses, and for the first time since they'd met, she could see his eyes.

When her stomach flipped at the sight of them—they crinkled at the sides as he patiently waited for her to finish her perusal, done with his own—she wished he'd brought the glasses again. His eyes were kinder than she thought they would be. They were also sharp, light, and the combination of that expression as well as his outfit...

It was a good thing she'd practiced her self-control. Fanning herself would have been inappropriate.

"What are you doing here?"

Dear Reader,

For as long as I can remember, Greece has been a dream holiday destination of mine. Last year, we finally made that dream come true. It was a magical moment every time we stepped onto a Greek island, and I knew I had to set a romance in this breathtaking place. The runaway groom-to-be, the distraught bride-to-be and two siblings coerced into dealing with the drama came a little later.

I loved writing Caleb and Piper into the beautiful Greek setting I was lucky enough to experience. Some of what they go through is eerily similar to what I went through (I say, as if I didn't write the book that way). But my favorite part of writing their story was having Caleb fall in love first and have no idea what to do about it. (I refuse to apologize for writing a pining hero!) Piper and Caleb have rough pasts, but the beauty of romance is that they'll have a happy future. Together. Once they get through those pesky obstacles I wrote them, anyway.

I hope you enjoy *Island Fling with the Tycoon*!

Therese

Island Fling with the Tycoon

Therese Beharrie

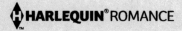

HARLEQUIN® ROMANCE

Recycling programs
for this product may
not exist in your area.

ISBN-13: 978-1-335-49953-0

Island Fling with the Tycoon

First North American publication 2019

Copyright © 2019 by Therese Beharrie

Printed in U.S.A.

Being an author has always been **Therese Beharrie**'s dream. But it was only when the corporate world loomed during her final year at university that she realized how soon she wanted that dream to become a reality. So she got serious about her writing, and now writes books she wants to see in the world featuring people who look like her for a living. When she's not writing, she's spending time with her husband and dogs in Cape Town, South Africa. She admits that this is a perfect life, and is grateful for it.

Books by Therese Beharrie

Harlequin Romance

Billionaires for Heiresses

Second Chance with Her Billionaire
From Heiress to Mom

Conveniently Wed, Royally Bound

United by Their Royal Baby
Falling for His Convenient Queen

The Tycoon's Reluctant Cinderella
A Marriage Worth Saving
The Millionaire's Redemption
Tempted by the Billionaire Next Door
Surprise Baby, Second Chance
Her Festive Flirtation

Visit the Author Profile page at Harlequin.com.

For Grant, who routinely helps me turn my dreams into reality.

Thank you for Greece.

And for our Greece group and the wonderful tour guides in Mykonos and Santorini.

Thank you for making a dream—and this book—possible.

CHAPTER ONE

FIVE MINUTES.

It wasn't long to wait. Things happened, even to drivers from five-star resorts. Or was it five-star accommodation? A five-star villa? Piper Evans wasn't sure. Her brother Liam had used all those terms when he'd told her she'd be staying there. The name of the place was Pleasure Villas, though that wasn't in any of the pictures he'd sent. Either way, Liam had hyped it up so much Piper could have sworn he was trying to get her to move to Greece rather than stay a week for his wedding.

But that was Liam. Or it had been Liam since they'd reconnected after their father's death. Enthusiastic, sincere. Responsible...? She wasn't entirely sure how to answer that. He hadn't been, once upon a time. He was getting married now, though, and marriage didn't exactly scream irresponsibility.

And yet she was still waiting at the airport for a driver he had been meant to arrange for her.

Ten minutes.

Why had she left the task to Liam anyway? She knew how he could be. She had countless examples of him letting her down. Sure, it seemed like he'd changed. The getting married thing, and all that. Or had she only wanted to believe that?

No, she thought. He *had* changed. Mostly since he'd met Emma, his fiancée, but still. Before their father had died, she and Liam had been in touch once, maybe twice a year. Then Liam had started dating Emma, and he'd been in touch more. Piper occasionally met up with them for meals. She wouldn't go so far as to say they were erasing the past, but this was a start. Enough of one that she could see how Emma influenced Liam.

Their relationship had lasted longer than any of Liam's previous ones. The one-year mark had come quickly, and he was still deeply in love. Then the engagement, planning a wedding—all within six months—and her brother wasn't running.

She tried not to feel resentment at that. Rather, she focused on the hope that surged inside her. Liam's relationship with Emma proved people could move forward regardless of their past. Maybe that meant she could, too. One day, she might finally be able to erase the marks her father had left on her life, her relationships, like Liam had.

Except it was now twenty minutes since she'd arrived, and her driver still wasn't there. Which meant her brother hadn't organised her a ride to the accommodation, as he'd assured her several times he had.

She let out a breath. Forcibly relaxed her clenched jaw. She searched the car park of the small Mykonos Airport, looking for anyone who could be looking for her. But, as had been the case for the past twenty minutes, no one seemed to be there without a purpose. She walked back through the sliding doors, circled the small waiting area. She saw only one person.

He'd been there when she'd landed. He held a sign that said Sunset Resort and wore a glowering expression behind dark sunglasses. Something about him made her shudder, and she was immensely glad she wasn't staying at Sunset Resort.

She pulled her eyes away from the stranger, sighed and pulled out her phone. She'd bought an international SIM card for this very reason.

Maybe you don't believe Liam has changed after all.

'Hello?'

'Liam,' she said, relief making her voice breathy. 'I'm so glad you answered.'

'Did something happen? Are you okay?'

'I'm fine.' She began walking to the sliding doors again, dragging her bag behind her. 'I've just been waiting for almost half an hour for the driver you arranged.'

'You have been?' he asked. 'That can't be right. Are you sure?'

'Considering I'm here alone—have been for the last thirty minutes—yes, I'm sure.'

'I'm sorry, Pie,' he said, using the name he'd given her as a child. She still hated it. 'Someone should have been there right when you landed. I gave Caleb your flight details. He's been tracking you, and there's no way he'd make you wait.'

'Caleb?' she said, wondering why the name sounded so familiar.

'Yeah, Caleb. Emma's brother.'

'Oh, *Caleb*,' she said again, as if she knew the man and hadn't only heard his name.

To be honest, Piper thought him a fantasy. Emma talked about her mysterious older brother whenever they got together, yet Piper had only met Emma's younger siblings. For all she knew, Emma had made up this mythical tale of the protective, kind older brother who'd taken care of them after their father died.

Piper had done that with Liam. When her father had refused to let her leave the house or made her jump through hoops when she wanted to study, she'd pretended Liam hadn't left home as soon as he'd got the chance. She'd told herself he was working hard to get her out of the situation he'd escaped.

She hadn't indulged such fantasies for long.

Maybe this wedding was finally the opportunity for reality to eclipse Emma's fantasy, too.

'Let me give him a call and find out what happened.'

'Okay.'

Liam hung up without saying goodbye, which would have bothered her more if he hadn't done so for her sake. A moment later, she heard a ringing from behind her. *Close* behind her. She turned. Found her head shifting up to look at the man with the sunglasses before he answered his phone.

'Caleb,' he said in a voice that made her skin feel prickly. He listened, then nodded. 'I have it handled.' He finished the call, though Piper could still hear speaking coming from the other end.

They looked at each other. Piper's heart began to pound. It jumped into her throat when her phone rang. She brought it to her ear without breaking eye contact.

'Yeah?'

'Pie, Caleb says he has it handled. I have no idea what that means, but—'

'It means he's here,' Piper interrupted. 'My ride's here.'

'Did you say *he's here*?' Liam asked, tone incredulous. 'As in, you think Caleb is there to pick you up?'

'Yes.'

'That can't be right.'

'Hold on.' She lowered her phone, pressing it to her chest. 'Are you Emma's Caleb?'

'Yes.'

'You're here to pick me up?'

'Yes.'

She narrowed her eyes. 'Yeah, it's him,' she said, speaking into the phone again. 'I'll see you soon.'

'Pie? Piper!'

'What?'

'Be careful.'

'Be…'

But her brother had already ended the call. This time, she didn't mind because she barely noticed he had.

He was having a day. Caleb Martin did not have days.

He had successes. Wins. But this morning the catering company his sister Emma had hired to cater the rehearsal party—because a dinner was too small for her grandiose wedding—had cancelled because some pop star had hired their services instead. Emma had come to him in a panic and, though Mykonos wasn't his home, Caleb had had to call in favours with every Greek contact he had to replace the caterer.

Since he didn't have that many Greek contacts, it had taken nearly all morning to find someone else. Then, as if sensing his vulnerability, his driver had handed in his resignation. Apparently, the demands of the wedding were too much for the local to handle. The man clearly wasn't used to responsibility.

Caleb hadn't had the choice. He'd been forced into duty the moment his father had died and he'd been made guardian of his three young siblings. Perhaps that was why he didn't have patience for the driver quitting. Or perhaps it was because the man had done so minutes before Liam's sister was supposed to land. With everyone running around preparing for the party that was two hours away, Caleb had no choice but to do it himself.

But she'd been late. Or not late, he thought, looking at the woman peering up at him. Confused. Though how she could be confused when he was the only man standing in the damn airport, Caleb had no idea.

'So, you're picking me up?' she said, bright brown eyes looking at him curiously. He couldn't figure out if they were light brown or dark brown, or a mysterious mixture of the two. All he knew was they stood out against her skin—another interesting shade of brown—and that they tempted him into forgetting his annoyance.

'Since I'm the only person in this airport with a sign,' he said, voice harder than he'd intended, 'the answer is obviously yes.'

She studied him before she answered. 'Two things. One, you're holding a sign that says Sunset Resort. The place I'm supposed to be staying at is called Pleasure Villas.'

Her cheeks turned a pretty pink colour. It almost distracted him from what she'd said. He looked down, cursed when he saw she was right. He'd grabbed the wrong sign from the seat of the car his driver had used.

Great.

'Two,' she continued as if she hadn't paused to make him feel like a fool, 'I was the only person standing out there for the last half an hour, too. If it was obvious that I should have noticed you, surely the same goes for you?' Her eyebrows rose. 'At least I have a legitimate excuse for not speaking to you. I didn't know you'd be coming. But what's your excuse? Didn't you at least look at a picture of me?'

No, he hadn't. Nor did he have an excuse, which she knew, based on that self-satisfied look on her face. He didn't know how he could find the arrogant expression appealing. How he could be fascinated by the easy curves of her lips. He hadn't even got to those intriguing eyes yet and he could feel his body leaning in, giving in to the desire to be closer to her.

He shut it down like a mousetrap on a mouse.

'If you're done, we can go.'

Amusement flickered in her eyes, but she was wise enough not to respond. She merely nodded and gestured for him to lead the way. He kept his complaints about the bad luck he was having to himself, though his mind went haywire, thinking about everything he should have been doing instead of fetching a snappy soon-to-be relative.

No, he thought immediately. She wouldn't be his relative. Good thing, too, or the way his body was still demanding to be closer to her would be criminal.

Grunting, he took the handle of her bag. When he was met with resistance, he looked at her.

'Is this going to be a problem?'

'You tell me,' she replied mildly. Which, of course, only annoyed him more.

'I'd like to help you with your bag,' he said through his teeth. 'Would you give me the great pleasure of doing so?'

Her expression changed then. So marginally that if his attention hadn't been focused on every twitch of her features he wouldn't have noticed it. Her lips pursed for a second; the lines around her eyes became more distinct. Tension fluttered across her face, disappearing almost as soon as it appeared.

When she looked at him, her eyes were dull. Inexplicably, his stomach dropped.

'Why?' she asked him, her voice steady despite the tension. 'Why do you want to carry my bag?'

'Not because I don't think you can do it,' he replied, watching her closely. It caused another minute change—a ripple of pleasure. But surely she couldn't take pleasure from him thinking she could do something as simple as carry her own bag? 'I help my sisters with their things all the time.'

'I'm not your sister.'

The words were soft. Softened something inside him, too. The annoyance went up another notch.

'No, you're not.' He waited a beat. 'Perhaps I wanted to be a gentleman.'

'Something tells me being a gentleman isn't a top priority for you.'

He didn't wince, but he wanted to. She was right. He'd been acting like a jerk since they'd met. But the knowledge of it didn't change that he was annoyed. That that annoyance wouldn't allow him to be soft and kind with her. Although it did give him an excuse to give her what she wanted. What, apparently, was important to her.

'Fine,' he said after a beat, releasing his hold on her bag. 'You can do it yourself. The car's this way.'

He walked away, pretending not to notice her shocked expression.

CHAPTER TWO

EMMA'S BROTHER WAS not quite as mythical as she'd made him seem. He was very much human, Piper thought, unashamedly studying him as he drove.

His jaw was locked, the sharp angles of it more pronounced because of the tension. Most of his expression was still obscured by his glasses, though she could tell he was glowering. The glasses seemed necessary for that—or, rather, the expression seemed necessary. She hadn't seen anything other than it since they'd met.

It wasn't her fault he'd had the wrong sign. And maybe she should have asked him, but she never approached strange men. She steered away from men in general, actually. Found it to be a good rule since she didn't trust her own judgement.

The first man she'd trusted had manipulated her whenever she'd allowed it. When she hadn't, too. The second man she'd trusted had abandoned her; she still hadn't forgiven her brother for that, if she was being honest. As for the third man...

She'd chosen Brad, and somehow he'd ended

up being exactly like her father. She'd paid for that. Was still paying for it in the form of caution and rules and the constant fear of falling for the wrong person again.

She sucked her lip in, looked out of the window. Her trip down memory lane had extinguished her curiosity about the man beside her. Instead, she focused on the actual lane they were driving along. It was an apt description for the narrow road they were rattling down. Caleb handled it with a confidence she wasn't sure the road warranted.

She wanted to tell him to slow down, to give way to the large buses driving the curves of the narrow road. To watch out for the scooters zooming past them at what felt like every turn. But her voice wouldn't work. She suspected it had something to do with feeling vulnerable, and the fact that she didn't want him to know she was.

It seemed to be an unofficial mark of their short relationship, this vulnerability. Her inability to speak because of it. Back at the airport, when he'd assumed she'd wanted him to carry her bag without asking, it had kept her from accusing him of taking control like the men in her past. It had also kept her from blurting out a thank you when he'd told her he believed she could do it herself, *unlike* the men in her past.

That difference was why she'd been surprised he'd given in so easily. Nevertheless, her entire body had braced for the argument she'd thought would come. They'd been inevitable before, with Brad. And he'd disguised control with gentleman-liness, which was part of why it had taken her years before she'd seen it. It wasn't the only reason, but still, she was careful because of it. She didn't take anything at face value any more. She couldn't trust herself to.

The car jerked to the side as a bus took a narrow corner wide. A sound escaped from her lips.

'We're fine,' he said curtly.

'I didn't say anything.'

'You made a noise.'

'It was involuntary.'

'We're still fine.'

'So you say,' she muttered, refusing to look out of the window on his side as the bus loomed over them.

'You shouldn't have come to Mykonos if you're afraid of tight roads.'

'I couldn't get out of it.'

'You tried?' he asked, surprise making his voice lighter.

'Everything. But Liam had an answer for every concern.' She looked at him. 'Some of that was because of you,' she said accusingly.

'I didn't do anything.'

'Aren't you paying for the extravagant wedding?'

'Well, yes, but—'

'I couldn't afford to come here by myself.' She sighed at the idea. 'It was a legitimate excuse. Then Emma's magical unicorn of a brother swoops in and suddenly I have no reason to back out.'

Caleb made a strangled sound that would have been amusing had another bus not rounded the corner. She hissed out a breath.

'You didn't learn your lesson from the first bus?' he asked darkly. 'We're fine. This is how people drive here.'

'Doesn't mean I have to like it.'

'That's true.'

He pulled back onto the road. She closed her eyes when it seemed as if he was still too close to the walls keeping them from falling off the edge of the cliff.

She had an intense wave of nostalgia for home. In Cape Town, South Africa, she had a choice about what kind of road she wanted to drive on. It wasn't the standard, these narrow and inclined roads. No, the standard was wide open spaces with plenty of lanes to feel safe in.

'Piper.'

She opened her eyes at the sound of her name. She hadn't expected it. Hadn't expected to like the way he said it either.

Piper.

She heeded the warning of her inner voice and steeled herself.

'What?'

'Worrying about traffic means you're missing the view.'

'I live in one of the most beautiful cities in the world. I've seen views.'

'Just look.'

She did, but reluctantly. Made sure he knew it, too, with a little exhalation and roll of her eyes. The sharp intake of breath she took once she looked out over the stone walls wasn't contrived though. She hadn't been lying when she'd told Caleb about the Cape Town views, but that didn't mean she couldn't appreciate new ones.

This one was particularly stunning, the vast blue ocean stretching out, broken up by rocks and islands in the far distance. On the island itself, white buildings stretched up at different layers, marked by the blue shutters she associated with Greece though she'd never been there before. Interspersed were stretches of brown land, green trees, pink flowers. It was striking and, she had to admit, it distracted her from the drive.

When they went down a curving gravel road she held her breath. Moments later he stopped the car, and she exhaled.

'What if the place had been further down?' he asked dryly.

'I probably would have fainted and you could have done the gentlemanly thing and left me in the car to fend for myself.'

There was a beat before she thought she heard him chuckle, but he climbed out of the car before she could check. Good thing, too. If she saw him smile, or do anything other than glower, she might have to pay attention to the buzzing that had been in her body since they'd met. At the moment, she was blissfully ignoring it.

She'd practised hard on that ability for the last two years. She was pleased it was working.

'Would you like me to get your bag out, or do you want to do it yourself?' he asked when she joined him at the back of the car.

Oddly, the question touched her. It made her feel...understood, though that made no sense.

'I'll do it,' she answered, to be safe.

She climbed in, pulled at the bag. Pulled again when it didn't budge. It took her a second to realise it was stuck. Panic made her fingers clumsy as she tried to loosen the bag. Pride prevented her from asking for help.

She waited for Caleb's sigh. For the dip of the car that told her he was coming in to help. To take over because, obviously, she couldn't be trusted to do anything herself.

This is why you should leave things to me, Pipe,' Brad had told her whenever something like this had happened. *'You can't do it by yourself.'*

It was funny that she'd heard versions of that from her father all her life. When Brad had outright said it though, she hadn't listened to the alarm going off in her head.

Gritting her teeth, she pulled with all her strength. The bag came loose, but the momentum had her falling back. A hand pressed against her back, but was removed as soon as she was steady. She got out of the car, her face burning despite the triumph of exiting with her bag.

'Nice job.'

She lifted her chin. 'Please don't make fun of me.'

'I wasn't,' he said sincerely.

There was a shriek from somewhere behind them, ending the conversation before she could think about why his answer warmed her.

'Caleb, you *did* it!' Emma exclaimed, launching herself at him as he turned to face her. 'The caterers arrived an hour ago and everything seems to be going smoothly.'

He pushed at a braid that had flown over her face when she finally let go of him, and smiled. 'Of course, Em. What choice did I have?'

'Ha,' she said, poking him in the stomach. Then her eyes moved to Piper and softened. 'Piper! It's so lovely to see you!'

Emma went to hug her future sister-in-law. Caleb expected Piper to wince. To put distance between her and his affectionate—sometimes overly so—sister. But she opened her arms and squeezed Emma tight. His heart squeezed, too. He ignored the sensation.

'Em, you look beautiful,' Piper said when she leaned back.

Emma beamed at her, smoothing the strapless blue dress she wore before flipping her hair over her shoulder. 'I still have to have these styled,' she said, lifting a free braid.

'And I have to have the whole of this styled,' Piper replied, waving a hand down her body.

Emma laughed.

'Em, it's less than an hour before the party starts,' Caleb said. 'You need to get your hair done and leave. Your guests will start to arrive soon and you and Liam have to be there.'

'Yeah, yeah,' Emma said, rolling her eyes good-naturedly. 'It's not like my hair is going to take long.'

'Is Jada doing it?' Caleb asked, thinking of his baby sister.

'Yes.'

'Then you need as much time as you can get.'

Emma's expression turned thoughtful. 'True.' She kissed Piper on the cheek before doing the same to Caleb. 'Show her to her room, please, Caleb. Liam's already at the beach, welcoming guests.'

She stuck her tongue out before Caleb could say anything, leaving behind a restlessness in the silence.

'You should probably show me to my room,' Piper said eventually.

He acquiesced without reply.

He heard her intake of breath when they walked onto the Pleasure Villas property. It was like when she'd seen the view of the ocean, the island of Mykonos earlier. A gasp at the beauty. So simple, too, as if she hadn't seen something like it before. Or perhaps as if she could still appreciate beauty like it, despite seeing it in her home, as she'd claimed.

But even he, jaded as he was when it came to beautiful places, appreciated Pleasure Villas. Tall white buildings with blue shutters surrounded a bright blue pool. At almost each of the assortment of buildings, green leaves and pink flowers pressed against the white paint. Some crept up, along pillars. Others stretched over from one building to another. The greenery around the pool created an oasis he'd never had the opportunity to enjoy, too concerned with privacy than to strive for relaxation.

He wondered if that would be the case for Piper. She seemed closed off, private, though her tongue was sharp. But then he thought of how eagerly she'd opened her arms to his sister, how she didn't seem to be hesitant or resistant with Emma, and he didn't know. His first impression of her was challenged by almost every other moment he spent with her. As someone who prided himself on reading people quickly and efficiently, he didn't like that she was such an enigma.

Then again, he wasn't buying property from her as he did in his business. That was where he relied on his people-reading skills. Perhaps he needed to calm down. Not that thinking that helped him *to* calm down.

'Here you go,' he said, taking the key from on top of the door frame and opening the door.

'You left the key there?'

'It's safe.'

'Hmm.'

It was the only comment she made as she pulled her bag into the house.

There was another gasp when she was inside, and he felt a strong sense of satisfaction. He'd done some work on the inside of the villas when he'd bought them. Not enough to change the feel of them, but enough that he could be proud when someone liked them.

It had been no small feat to get Adrian Anagnos to sell this place to him. In Mykonos, businesses remained locally owned for the most part. There were none of the fast food places that had taken over most of Europe. Most of the restaurants and properties were family owned. It was how Mykonos had survived the recession, a fact they were quite proud of.

When he'd learnt of this, Caleb had been determined to get a foot in the door. He'd worked with

Adrian when the man had come to South Africa, interested in investing in property. Their relationship had been purely professional until, one day, Adrian's daughter had been robbed in Cape Town. Adrian had been in America on business. With no one else to assist her, Adrian had called Caleb, who hadn't given it a second thought.

Things changed then. Adrian invited Caleb on a boat trip one day in Cape Town to thank him. Dinner became more frequent, and Adrian became a mentor. Caleb didn't use that term lightly—it felt like a betrayal to his father, whose business Caleb had taken over when Chad Martin had died thirteen years ago. But Caleb had grown to like and respect Adrian. The older man felt the same about Caleb.

When Adrian had invited Caleb to Greece for his daughter's wedding, Caleb had stayed at this very property. It was one of several Adrian owned on the island. Caleb had liked it so much he'd enquired about purchasing it. It had taken two years before he'd finally worn Adrian down. Eventually, the man had stopped laughing at Caleb; now, Caleb was the owner. It was a deep disappointment that Adrian couldn't make Emma's wedding.

'This is… Wow,' Piper said, drawing him from his thoughts.

'Yeah, I thought the same thing when I first saw it.'

Piper ran a hand over the couch, looking from the cobbled tiling up to the sea-themed décor. She took the two steps up to the open-plan kitchen, walked out to the small courtyard at the back, then into the main bedroom with its en-suite bathroom. With wide eyes she walked out and stared at him.

'Are all the rooms in the villa like this?'

'Pretty much, yeah.'

'Wow,' she said again, setting her hands on the small blue table in the kitchen. 'How could you afford to rent this place?'

His lips twitched. 'I didn't rent it.'

She gave him a look. 'Liam told me you arranged for accommodation.'

'Technically true, although I didn't have to arrange much. I simply didn't hire it out for this week.'

'You didn't...'

He could see her brain working as she trailed off. Enjoyed that brief moment of shock when she realised what he meant.

'You own this place?'

She spoke in a whisper. He smiled.

'I do.'

'Holy cow.' She blinked. Repeated the action in rapid movements. 'I...guess I understand why Emma went so extravagant with the wedding now.'

'Liam wanted the wedding to be big, too,'

Caleb reminded her, as if he had to defend his younger sister.

'Yeah, but Liam wanted it because Emma wanted it.'

'Why do you sound so judgemental?'

'I'm not judging anyone,' she said, straightening her spine. 'I'm only saying that if I had access to literal paradise—' she lifted a hand, gestured around them '—I'd want to have a big destination wedding, too.'

'You're definitely judging her.'

She met his eyes. 'If you tell me you've never once judged Liam because of his choices, personal or professional, I'll tell you the truth about whether I'm judging her.'

Caleb thought back to all the things he'd seen Liam do—things he hadn't agreed with. Two failed business ventures in the year and a half since he and Emma had started dating. A lack of a spine when it came to even the vaguest prospect of conflict.

The only reason Caleb had felt comfortable with the wedding going ahead as planned was because Liam was completely in love with Emma. And he made Emma happy. Otherwise, Caleb might have had to step in, like his father would have, had the man still been alive...

Piper was smiling when he looked at her again.

'I'm going to get ready for the party. Please close the door on your way out.'

* * *

Piper dusted a hand over the olive-green dress she wore. It was simple, with thin straps, and revealed more of her breasts than she'd ever shown before. But it had pockets, ended mid-shin, and the colour popped against her skin. She couldn't bring herself to change, despite the situation with her breasts.

She lifted her hand to her hair, which she'd had to tie up into a ponytail since she'd worn it that way on the flight over. There had been no time to wash and blow it again. She'd tied it up, flattened the front of it with gel and straightened her ponytail until it was a sleek curtain to her mid-back. With one last look in the mirror, she grabbed her clutch and opened the door.

Right to Caleb Martin.

They both took a step back. Both sized each other up in the silence that followed. He wore light blue pants and a white shirt. It accentuated the brown of his skin, the broadness of his shoulders, the dark black of his hair. He'd shaved since they last saw one another, so the sharp angles of his face were even more striking than they'd been that afternoon. Or perhaps that was because he no longer wore sunglasses, and for the first time since they'd met she could see his eyes.

When her stomach flipped at them—they crinkled at the sides as he patiently waited for her to finish her perusal, done with his own—she wished he'd brought the glasses again. His eyes were kinder than she'd thought they would be. They were also sharp, light, and the combination of that expression as well as his outfit…

It was a good thing she'd practised her self-control. Fanning herself would have been inappropriate.

'What are you doing here?' she asked when she was finally done staring. No, that wasn't true. She wasn't done. She simply knew what was proper.

'Emma asked me to escort you to the party.'

'Why? Is it complicated to get to the beach?'

'It is not.' Amusement shimmered across his face, a potent addition to the gorgeousness she was already distracted by.

'Is she trying to set us up?'

His eyes widened comically, the determined shake of his head following in a similar manner. 'No. No, of course not.'

'You're denying this a lot.'

'Doesn't mean it's not true.'

It would probably annoy him if she disagreed— so, of course, that was what she wanted to do. She walked out of the door, closed it behind her. Primly, she folded her hands around her clutch.

'I don't know. You came to fetch me from the airport. You showed me to my room. Now you're escorting me to a party. This must be a date of some sort.'

'It's not a date,' he said. 'It's…being courteous. Which I'm deeply regretting.'

'You're the least courteous person I've met, Caleb. You telling me you regret being courteous proves that.'

'Has anyone ever pointed out how contrary you are?'

Why can't you do as you're told, Piper?

A question she'd heard far too often in her twenty-six years, in various forms.

'All the time,' she said lightly. Fighting for that tone. 'Though you think it an insult. It's not. I try to be contrary whenever I can, so someone pointing it out to me is a compliment. Shall we?'

She started walking, not bothering to check if he was following. She could almost hear his irritation with her. It thrilled her in a way it shouldn't have.

To be fair, some of what she'd said had been for the sake of contrariness—he was so easily riled!—but some of it had been true, too. She'd spent most of her life obeying people. Her mother had died when she was young, leaving her and her brother with a father who didn't want to be one. Keaton Evans had never said so, but she could only assume that was the reason for his awfulness. People who wanted children didn't force them into behaving in certain ways, did they? Surely they allowed their children to become whoever they wanted to be. They let them test the boundaries, drawing them in when the child went too far.

But not Keaton.

Keaton had a strict routine for them to follow. So strict, in fact, that if either of them strayed from it they were punished. No outside time. Food in their rooms. Being kept separate from one another. Since they had no friends, not really, Piper and Liam had become friends. At least they had been in those first few years. Not talking to one another was torture then, which their father knew. It was how he'd kept them in line.

There was no testing the boundaries in the Evans house. There were *only* the boundaries. If they were broken, Piper or Liam would be punished. At least Keaton had been simple in his cruelty.

As they'd got older, Liam began to rebel more, and things got bad. Eventually, Liam had got a bursary to university and moved out. Their father had forbidden him from coming back. Forbidden her from seeing him. They'd lost touch, even when she'd joined Liam at university two years later. By then she'd allowed her father to crush her spirit of rebellion. Of independence. She'd only got it back three years later, when Keaton had died.

Then she'd welcomed another manipulator into her life.

'It's hard to insult someone who doesn't have

the decency to be insulted by things that normal people are insulted by,' Caleb commented from beside her. She hadn't even noticed he'd caught up. Now that she had, she could feel his presence like the light breeze caressing her skin.

'That's the point,' she replied. 'I don't get insulted, and that way I take away the power from the person trying to insult me.'

'Sounds like you've practised it.'

'I have,' she told him simply, before stopping at the top of a steep decline. She let out a breath. 'I knew these heels were a bad idea.'

'I wouldn't say so,' his voice rumbled.

Her flesh shot out in goosebumps. And she remembered, for the first time, that she'd forgotten to put on the nipple covers she'd bought for the dress when she'd realised she couldn't wear a bra with it. She resisted angling her body away so he wouldn't know the effect his flirtatious remark had on her. It would be giving him power. On principle, she couldn't allow that.

'Well, I do,' she said determinedly. 'How am I supposed to make it down this path without breaking an ankle?'

'Take them off.'

She wrinkled her nose. 'Then I'd have dirty feet when I have to wear my shoes again.'

'You could wipe them off.'

'That won't help.'

He stared at her for a moment. 'You're strange.'

'Tell me something I don't know.'

'Well,' he said, 'you do have another option, though I don't think you're going to like it.'

'What is it?'

He turned to face her, his expression so satisfied that she wanted to give him whatever answer he didn't expect from her. Until she heard his suggestion.

'I could carry you.'

CHAPTER THREE

HE'D DONE IT on purpose. He wanted to ruffle her feathers when she seemed so composed. Perhaps not his most honourable decision in life, but he'd been honourable enough. When his father had died thirteen years before, he'd stepped up and taken care of his siblings, who'd been eleven, nine and seven years old. He'd only been eighteen at the time—he'd been the result of a teen pregnancy, the cause of a quickie marriage, and his parents had only had his siblings once they were more settled—and he'd been forced into being a guardian and entrepreneur when he'd taken over his father's business.

So he could afford a little dishonour. Particularly when it came to a woman who intrigued him.

Piper stared at him, those beautiful eyes big and bright and bold against the odd green of her dress. If he'd seen that shade in a store somewhere, he wouldn't have taken a second look. Or he might have, but only to be offended by it. Now, though, on Piper… It made her skin look as if it had been bronzed. And it flattered a body he'd been trying not to pay attention to since they'd met.

Her breasts were full and out on display, though he was trying not to pay attention to them either. He wasn't sure if it was because it would get him into trouble if he did, or if he was trying to be polite. But the straps of her dress rested over smooth, strong shoulders, the waist of it clinging to her ribcage then flaring out. The heels he'd teased her about earlier did excellent things to the legs the dress revealed, though there wasn't much of them to see.

She wore no jewellery, only the lightest of make-up, and the way her hair was tied up accentuated the angles of her face. It made her look innocent, despite her pink lips curving. Despite her high cheekbones, almost demanding her eyes to crinkle even when she wasn't smiling. When she did and those cheeks lifted, her eyes narrowing… He'd learnt his lesson after the first time. Now, he simply braced for the breath he'd lose.

'You're teasing me.'

'Maybe,' he answered.

'Not maybe—yes.' Her eyes flickered to his face before moving back to the steep path. 'This is payback for me not being offended by you.'

'What is?' he asked innocently. 'This decline? I don't control landscape, my dear.'

'Don't call me that,' she said, though her words lacked heat. 'It's condescending.'

'It's not. "My dear" is a phrase of affection.'

She snorted. 'Now I know you're being condescending. You certainly do *not* feel affection towards me.'

He wasn't sure how to respond. The truth was there was a slight niggling in his chest that made him feel something for her. He didn't know if it was affection or if he'd merely suppressed his annoyance.

'Okay.'

He blinked. 'What?'

'Okay, carry me.' She stepped closer to him, giving him a whiff of a scent that reminded him of wild flowers. 'You're still offering, aren't you?'

'I— Yes, of course.' He cleared his throat. Did it again.

She smirked. 'Something wrong, Caleb?'

In one quick movement he scooped her into his arms. Her hands went around his neck with a quick exhalation, and he caught the smell of mint on her breath. It made his body tingle—though that might have been due to the fact that she fitted in his arms perfectly. He tried not to think about the soft flesh of her thighs against his bottom arm, or his hand on her perfect waist.

While he was at it, he resisted the desire to put his nose in her neck, to get more of that intoxicating perfume she was wearing. Or did she simply smell that way? Could someone's natural scent be this heady?

Caleb.

He kept himself from groaning now, too. His entire body had gone tense from the control he was exerting. But he thought of all the times he'd had to exercise control in his life. It was interchangeable with responsibility in his family, it seemed. Like during that phase when Tate, his brother, had refused to eat anything besides pizza. Caleb had refrained from buying anything else— including pizza—if Tate didn't eat at least one nutritional meal a day. There'd been a week where things had been touch and go, but it had worked out.

Then there was that time Jada had consistently got up late for school. No matter what Caleb had done, they'd arrived anywhere from fifteen to thirty minutes late. Jada had got detention and Caleb had received numerous notes about punctuality. Eventually, he'd refused to put the hot water on in the mornings if she didn't get up by six. He'd stood guard over the switch since it meant the entire house didn't get warm water. After three days of the Martin siblings going to school without showers, the collective effort of him, Emma and Tate had forced Jada to get up on time.

He smiled at the memory.

'You're enjoying this?'

It took the question to realise his trip down

memory lane had distracted him from the woman in his arms. Now that she'd spoken, he realised it wouldn't work again.

'No.' He took the first tentative step down the hill. Once he got his grip, he took another. 'I was thinking about how my sister's getting married.'

'No, you weren't.' She continued before he got the chance to ask how she knew. 'What are you feeling about it?'

'Affectionate. Nostalgia.'

'That's it?'

He looked down. 'What are you feeling?'

'I don't know.' There was silence as he took the next few steps. 'I'm happy for Liam and Emma. They obviously care about one another. Liam's changed a lot since they've met.'

Caleb tried not to snort at that. Piper narrowed her eyes.

'See, you're not only feeling affection and nostalgia. You don't like my brother?' she asked after a beat.

'I do.' He took a breath, another step. 'It's not that I don't like him. I certainly wouldn't have allowed him to marry my sister if I didn't like him.'

Her body stiffened. Even when he looked down at her, saw her face taut, saw her actively try to relax it, he still felt her tight muscles in her arms.

'What?' he asked. 'What did I say wrong?'

Her eyes met his. There was an inexplicable disappointment there. His stomach turned.

'Nothing,' she replied. A bald-faced lie. They both knew it. Neither of them addressed it. 'Are we done?' she asked quietly a moment later. Caleb turned, saw they were, and lowered her gently.

'I didn't mean to upset you,' he said when she was on the ground again.

'It's fine.'

'It's not fine, clearly.'

'It's not fine,' she told him, giving him a sad smile. 'But it doesn't matter.'

He wanted to tell her it did, but he had no reason to. He locked his jaw. Didn't bother prying it open when she'd obviously made up her mind. Nothing he could say would make her more receptive to his words. He was sure of it because that stubborn furrow in her brow told him she didn't only feel sad.

He started walking again, along the narrow path that led to the beach. It was covered with sand, more so the closer they got, but he didn't turn around to offer assistance. If she wanted to be stubborn, she'd have to deal with the consequences of it.

Again, not his most honourable decision, but something about Piper rubbed him up the wrong way.

Or the right way.

He grunted at the voice in his head. He didn't need a reminder of the attraction he felt for her. He could still feel her body in his arms. Could still smell her. Still had the desire to bury his nose in her neck. Maybe brush her pink lips when he drew back, taste that mouth, the curve of it—

His thoughts abruptly stopped when he got to the beach. There were people here and if he continued down that path he'd surely embarrass himself in front of all of them. He glanced over his shoulder to check that she was still okay. She seemed to be, though the pull of her lips made him think she wasn't pleased.

Good. Neither was he.

He grabbed a glass of champagne from the nearest waiter and drank.

Piper had to give it to Emma and Liam: extravagance could be quite beautiful.

Once she'd got over being left to fend for herself down that sandy path—which, in hindsight, was probably fair. What could he have done, carried her the entire way?—she was able to enjoy it.

The setting was magnificent. An entire stretch of the beach had been reserved for the party, which allowed for generous decorations. Emma and Liam had taken advantage. A large portion of the beach had been covered in wooden planks. A long table sat on the planks, decorated with greenery and candles, along with a bar and round cocktail tables.

On the sand beyond it were wooden squares, stacked and decorated to form smaller tables. The

area was full of them, scattered with round com-
fortable-looking cushions as seats. Candles and
fairy lights illuminated the area, which would
need the light in a few moments. Currently, the
sun was lowering in the sky, casting an orange
glow over the ocean. It was breathtaking.

'Pretty, isn't it?'

Jada, Emma's younger sister, came to stand beside her. She was a picture in a light blue dress,
her short hair straight around her face, large navy
earrings in her ears.

'It is,' Piper said with a smile. 'So are you.'

Jada blushed. 'You're just saying that.'

'I happen to mean it. But what does it matter if
I'm just saying it?' she asked, bumping her shoulder against the young woman's. 'I'm surprised
you were allowed to wear blue.'

Jada laughed. 'I had to. Not the same shade as
Emma's dress, of course, but since Emma wanted
the wedding's theme to be "shades of blue" this
worked.'

'It certainly does.'

Piper scanned the small crowd. Most of the
people she didn't recognise. Her mother had been
an only child and she and Liam had never got
along with their father's siblings or their children.
Unsurprisingly, Liam hadn't wanted them at his
wedding. Surprisingly, he had wanted her there.

She supposed that might be too harsh. They'd
seen each other often enough in the last five years

that her invitation was warranted. The surprise? That was her resentment talking. Her memories of how he'd abandoned her to fend for herself for two years.

It slipped in, even when she was trying to be positive.

The truth was that if it hadn't been an all-expenses-paid trip to a Greek island during the school holidays when she wasn't teaching, Piper would have stayed at home. In some ways then, she was glad she'd been forced to be there. She needed to move on. Her father was dead. Had been for five years. That time long surpassed the time she'd spent alone with her father after Liam had left. She had to let it go.

She wasn't sure why she couldn't.

'Where are they?' she asked suddenly, not seeing them in the crowd.

'Over there.'

Jada pointed to a section of the beach that wasn't a part of the evening's celebrations. Piper clearly saw the two of them—Emma in her blue dress, Liam in a blue shirt and black pants—but something about it didn't feel right.

'Are they…are they arguing?'

Jada sighed. 'For the last ten minutes.'

'Did something happen?'

'Nothing I can think of. I mean, Em did get really quiet while I was doing her hair, but I thought that was nerves.'

'Cold feet?' Piper wondered out loud.

'I don't think so. I'm sure Emma would have said something. She's not exactly a great keeper of secrets.'

Piper studied the couple. It was clear they were arguing. Her brother's shoulders were squared back, as they always were when he felt attacked. She'd grown used to the stance. Had used it as a warning sign to stay out of his and their father's way.

'You're staring,' a quiet voice said from her side.

Piper turned to see Tate join them. He followed their gaze.

'You are, too, dummy,' Jada said without heat. Her tone was laced with worry.

'It's obvious.'

'Should one of us go check it out?'

'No,' came a new voice. Piper hadn't needed Caleb to answer his sister's question to know he was there. She'd felt him join their group. Her heart had sped up. Her body had become a little more aware. 'Let's give them a moment to sort this out.'

There was a long silence as they heeded the instruction. Piper didn't do so happily. She was worried by the disappointment that had washed over her earlier. When he'd spoken about 'allowing' Emma and Liam to marry. Before that moment, she'd almost forgotten she wasn't supposed to be interested in him. She'd been too distracted by the easy strength of his arms. By how he didn't only seem to be carrying her because he'd provoked her, but because he was a nice person.

But nice people weren't controlling. That trait reminded her too much of her father for her to make that evaluation. It was too much like her ex-boyfriend, too. The blurred lines with Caleb meant she needed to keep her distance. She couldn't repeat the mistakes of her past. She couldn't let her mind linger on *niceness*.

'Should we stop staring?' Jada asked into the quiet.

'Yes,' Piper replied. No one moved.

Then it happened.

Liam's hand paused as it ran through his hair, before dropping with such a force Piper didn't know how it hadn't taken him to the floor. Emma took a step forward. Liam didn't move. She took another, resting her hands on his chest. Liam stepped back. There was a beat. Then her brother turned and ran.

Through the tables on the sand, past the wooden planks and all the guests who were there to celebrate with him and Emma. Past his future in-laws, who were staring at him in bewilderment. Past Piper, who watched him with a sinking feeling in her stomach.

But not surprise. No, not surprise.

Moments later, they all watched as Liam

jumped onto the dock, onto a boat that had just been untied. He exchanged a few words with the man at the helm. Soon he was gone.

An uncomfortable silence settled. Then came Jada's trembling voice.

'Did he…did he just run away from Emma?'

CHAPTER FOUR

SHE WAS GOING to kill her brother. She'd make it swift, painless, because he was family. But he deserved death for this. Running away from his fiancée on the evening of their rehearsal dinner. Four days before their wedding.

Since she was the only one of his family there, it automatically put her in the spotlight. Taking in the three pairs of eyes staring at her, she finalised the plans for his death.

'Did your brother run away from our sister?' Jada demanded now, a clear distinction between *them* and Piper in that question.

'I was watching, same as you were,' Piper said with a calm she didn't feel. Her heart was pounding in her ears. She forced herself to take a breath when she realised she'd stopped inhaling and exhaling.

'Why?' Tate asked.

'Why was I watching with you?'

'Why would your brother leave our sister?'

'Tate.'

Caleb spoke softly, but the twenty-year-old reared back as if his brother had shouted. They exchanged a look, and when Tate looked back at Piper there was shame in his eyes. She wasn't sure if she felt sorry for him or if she was impressed at Caleb's nonverbal abilities.

'Do you have any idea what happened?' Caleb asked her.

'This is the first time I've seen my brother since arriving. I have no idea. But you know who does?'

She gestured to where Emma was standing. The Martin siblings' heads collectively turned, looking in that direction, as if they'd just realised she was still there. They all moved towards her, before Caleb stretched out an arm, stopping his siblings.

'At least one of us has to stay here.'

'Tate will,' Jada said.

At the same time Tate said, 'Jada.'

Caleb lifted a brow. They both sighed.

'Fine.'

'I can stay,' Piper offered, suddenly wanting to make herself useful.

The bond between the siblings was obvious, and it was making her nostalgic for something that had never been in her past. Or perhaps it had, after their mother had died and she and Liam had still sought comfort with one another.

'No,' Caleb said. 'They will. Help smooth everything over here, distract people. Pretend like what Liam did and everyone saw was part of the plan.'

'What should I do?' she asked in a small voice, emotion hammering into her like a battering ram. It broke down the defences she'd put in place, and she couldn't fight her instincts without them. Unfortunately, those instincts had been built and honed during her childhood. When she'd reverted to her father because he'd demanded she do so.

'Come with me,' Caleb said, interrupting her thoughts. 'You're his family. You deserve to know what happened.'

She didn't think she agreed with that, but she was touched by the sentiment. Enough that she obeyed, ignoring the whirlwind inside her. The war, really, between the part of her wondering if she was obeying because she wanted to or if it meant she was doing it again.

She'd ignored her feelings with Brad, had obeyed. Things had snowballed during their relationship. Two years later, she was still cold from being buried under the avalanche.

She wrapped her arms around herself, hoping to hide the shudder that had gone through her body. Caleb didn't seem to be paying attention to her though. His eyes were on Emma, her hunched-over frame keeping his focus. She glanced back at where she'd seen her brother disappear. The boat was gone, the ocean calm, as if the turmoil of the last few minutes hadn't happened.

You'd better have a reason for running, Liam, Piper told him silently.

Emma went into his arms the moment they reached her. His heart ached and he tightened his hold before leaning back, keeping his hands on her arms.

'We saw what happened, but a lot of the guests didn't,' he said, knowing his sister needed him to take control. All of his siblings needed him to, in emergencies. 'I told Tate and Jada to pretend it was part of the evening's festivities. If you'd prefer we tell the truth, we'll do that. But I wanted to give you a moment to recover before you have people rushing to your side.'

Emma's lip wobbled but she nodded, stepping out of his embrace and straightening her shoulders. Pride filled him. He folded his arms to keep from reaching out to her anyway.

'What happened?' he asked after he'd given her a moment.

'He ran.'

'Yes, we know that. But you were fighting before. What about?'

She pursed her lips, taking a shaky breath. 'He has cold feet.'

Caleb barely kept himself from growling.

'We made an offer on a place back in Cape

Town and the estate agent called to say they accepted the offer. It freaked him out.'

'So he ran?' Caleb asked, incredulous. He wanted to wring Liam's neck.

'Well, he started freaking out. Pacing. Breathing quick.' She dug a heel into the sand. 'It made me freak out and…and I told him something that made him run.'

'What?'

Her eyes met Piper's. Piper looked back steadily. For some reason, it made Emma's eyes fill. Before he could curse that he didn't have a tissue for her, Piper handed Emma one.

'Thanks,' she said, blowing her nose. She took a deep breath. 'He isn't ready for marriage.'

'What are you talking about?' Caleb demanded. 'He asked you to marry him. Hell, he asked *me* if he could marry you, which we both know takes guts.'

Piper blinked at him in surprise. He merely lifted his shoulders.

'He loves you, Emma,' Caleb said with a shake of his head. 'There's no way he doesn't want to marry you.'

If he didn't, Caleb would kill him. Then bring him back from the dead and force him to do right by Emma.

'It's true,' Piper said softly. It was the first thing she'd said since they'd arrived. He supposed he should be happy she'd contributed at all. He was particularly happy she'd contributed with this.

Emma breathing began to sound like sobs. Caleb angled his body to keep her from the guests' view. Piper did the same.

'He panicked,' Emma said. 'About the house and—' She broke off again.

'It's a big commitment,' Piper said. 'Especially for him.'

'I know. But I didn't force him to marry me. I didn't give him an ultimatum or anything. I didn't even tell him I wanted to buy a house.'

The more Emma spoke, the guiltier Caleb felt. He should have asked more questions. Done more than a credit check on Liam. He hadn't protected Emma, and now she was hurt. What kind of a brother did that make him? What kind of a father figure? He could almost hear his father's voice from the grave, asking him those questions. Hell, if his father had been here, this probably wouldn't have happened.

He quelled the guilt with anger.

'Did he force you to do this, Em?'

'What? No, no. No,' she said again. 'I wanted to do all this.'

'You signed the pre-nup, didn't you?'

'Caleb,' Emma said sharply, her first show of emotion apart from devastation, 'Liam wasn't doing this for the money.'

He didn't reply.

'Really.' Emma's voice softened. 'He ran because…because I'm pregnant, and it freaked him out. We never spoke about starting a family, and I think because of how he grew up…with your father,' she said to Piper, 'I think he's scared to be one. Or he doesn't know what kind of father he'll be. I don't know. I… I…'

She started crying in earnest now, and Caleb set aside his shock and admonishments—hadn't he had the sex talk with all his siblings; what didn't they understand about possible pregnancy and STDs?—and drew her into a hug. Her body shook in his arms. His heart shook along with it. And he got more and more upset. More determined that he should have protected her from a man who could be so careless with her heart. Guiltier that he hadn't acted like their father would have.

'Em,' Caleb said softly, running a hand over her hair. 'It's going to be okay.'

She said something, but it was muffled since she was crying into his chest. He looked at Piper, who was staring at them both a little helplessly. He knew it was irrational, but he was suddenly angry with her, too.

She should have warned Emma her brother would be so reckless. She should have warned *him* at the very least. He could have warned Emma. Banned her from seeing Liam. Anything to keep this moment from happening.

Then she met his eyes and his heart flipped at the pain he saw there. At the extent of that helplessness. Something about it made him want to reach out and take her into his arms, too. Involuntarily, his muscles spasmed. Emma drew back and looked at them both. Her make-up was still flawless. He was glad that ridiculously priced make-up artist they'd hired was worth the money.

'You have to find him,' she said, blinking up at him. 'Please. He's scared, and I'm worried he'll do something dangerous.' She looked at Piper. 'You know why he did this. He needs you to bring him back.'

'He… I…' Piper stammered. She gave a quick shake of her head. 'No, Emma. He doesn't need me.'

'He might,' Emma said softly. 'He definitely needs me. He just doesn't know it yet.'

Caleb admired his sister's quiet resolve. He didn't appreciate that it was days before her wedding, and it came courtesy of a runaway groom.

'Emma—'

'Please,' his sister interrupted, aiming the full force of her puppy dog eyes at Piper. He silently wished Piper luck. He hadn't been able to resist that look since…ever. 'Please bring him back.'

'I… Okay,' Piper said hesitantly.

'Thank you,' Emma said, hugging Piper. Then she broke away from Piper and drew him into a hug. 'Thank you, Caleb.'

'Why are you thanking me?' he asked, though he patted Emma's back.

She aimed the puppy dog eyes at him now. 'Because you're going with Piper. You're going to help her find Liam.'

CHAPTER FIVE

'THIS EVENING DID not go like I thought it would,' Piper said.

It was after everything had ended at the rehearsal dinner. Jada and Tate had woven an elaborate tale about Liam going hunting for the perfect wedding gift on one of the Greek islands. Caleb and Piper had returned without Emma, assuring her they'd make something up about her disappearance, too.

They'd stumbled through an excuse. Something about her joining Liam on his excursion. He didn't think many people believed them—some of them had seen the argument and, of course, rumours had spread—but then the entertainment had arrived and they'd been distracted.

The dinner had gone on as planned without the bride and groom. He and Piper had sat at the designated seats to make their emptiness less conspicuous. It had only succeeded in making *him* feel more conspicuous. He was certain it had nothing to do with how it made it look as if he and Piper were getting married.

'You can say that again,' he said, lowering to join her on the planks. He'd grabbed two bottles from the bar on his way there, and only now saw what they were. 'I have a cider and beer. I'm not sure which one you want.'

'Cider,' she said. She waited for him to open it. 'Nice of you to think of me.'

'It's been a long night. Figured we needed it.'

She clinked her bottle against his. They drank in silence for a few minutes.

'Do you think Emma's going to be okay?'

'What do you think?' he asked, a little too harshly.

'This isn't my fault, you know,' she said after a beat. 'Liam is his own person. He makes his own decisions. I had nothing to do with him leaving.'

She was right, and he was desperately trying to figure out why he was holding her accountable for her brother's actions. Was it because that was what he'd done his entire life? He'd taken responsibility for his siblings' actions even though he had no control over what they did?

But that was family, he thought. That was what his father had taught him about being part of a family. Long before his mother had left, overwhelmed by the responsibilities of being a parent of four when his siblings had come in quick succession, his father had taught them they were a unit. They looked out for one another.

When his father had died in a freak accident inspecting a property under construction, Caleb had felt that responsibility more than ever. It didn't matter that he hadn't felt capable of parenting three kids. He'd barely been an adult himself; had just finished school. But he'd stepped up. He knew it was what his father would have wanted. And there was no way he was going to let his siblings go into the system.

He only hoped it made up for how he hadn't taken his father's teachings seriously when the man had been alive.

'I know,' he answered, taking a long drag from his beer.

'Do you?' she asked. 'I feel like you're judging me. Or treating me like I told Liam to run away instead of face his responsibilities.'

Something in her tone made him look at her. Something on her face confirmed his suspicions.

'He's done this before, hasn't he?'

She took a deep breath, set aside the cider. It was barely touched. For a long time she didn't speak. The only sounds were the staff clearing up around them. A few people lingered, but not close to them. Instead, they chose to explore the beach further down. Lights flickered in the distance, the faint sound of music vibrating through the air.

'He hasn't run from his responsibilities,' she said. 'I'm not his responsibility.'

'He ran from you?'

'Didn't you hear what I said?' she asked quietly. 'I'm not his responsibility so, technically, he didn't run from me.'

'Since when do technicalities matter when it comes to family?'

She angled her head, as if accepting his words. She didn't verbalise the acceptance.

'I will say that he runs from hard things,' she said after a moment. 'I imagine this experience has been hard for him. Then finding out he's about to become a father...'

She fell silent.

'You don't run away from hard things,' Caleb said firmly. 'Not from family or responsibilities. You face them.'

'*You* do, maybe. It's not as easy for the rest of us.'

He looked at her. 'What are you running away from, Piper?'

There was a beat. 'I wasn't talking about me. I was talking about Liam.'

He didn't call her out on her lie. Figured she'd told it to him for a reason. The same went for when he'd carried her down that path that afternoon. He was still dying to know what had happened then. But Piper didn't offer information for the sake of it. At least not about herself.

'Piper—'

'Look!' she interrupted him, jumping up and pointing into the distance. He could only hear the motoring of a boat, but when he stood he could see one that looked familiar.

'How did you know—?'

He cut himself off when he saw her lowering to take off the shoes she'd refused to remove earlier. Then she was running. Sprinting, actually, towards the dock.

A variety of scenarios went through his head. One was that if Liam had come back on that boat, Caleb would kill him. Two was that he couldn't let Piper go down there alone. They had no idea what they would face, or who would be there. And they were in a foreign country, for heaven's sake. One where they didn't speak English as their first language. Cursing, he ran after her.

She was already speaking to a guy on the dock by the time he arrived.

'I'm sorry, I don't know who you're talking about.'

The guy's English was perfect, though he had a slight Greek accent.

Caleb stepped forward. 'You're sure you didn't take a tourist anywhere today?'

The man shook his head. Caleb sighed, took out his wallet and a stack of euros.

'I'll give you all this if you tell me where he is.'

The stranger considered it for all of twenty seconds, before taking the cash from Caleb, counting it and pocketing it.

'I dropped him off at the other end of the island.'

'This island?' Caleb asked. 'He's still on the island?'

'He said he needed some things.'

Caleb turned to Piper. 'There's no way he went back to the villa.'

'Why not?' Piper asked, though mutedly, he thought. 'Everyone would have been at the party. We were comforting Emma for a long time. He could have come and gone and no one would be any the wiser.'

'But where would he go?'

'He asked about ferries when I dropped him,' the guy offered. 'I saw him walking to the ticket counter.'

Caleb studied the man, hoping his gaze would show how unimpressed he was that he'd only been given that information now.

'So he bought a ticket.'

'Where to?' Piper asked.

'That's the question,' Caleb said. He wondered how the hell he was going to tell Emma her fiancé had bought a ticket off the island. He shook his head. It wasn't an option.

He formulated a plan, thanked the man and walked a few metres before waiting for Piper to join him.

'We should go talk to the person at the ticket stall.'

'Good idea,' she said. 'You should do that.'

'Great,' he said, relieved she'd agreed. He'd been prepared for a fight. Then his brain caught up. 'Wait—did you say *I* should do that?'

'Yes.' Her gaze didn't waver. 'You've taken charge of this whole thing anyway. Giving instructions, asking the questions.'

'What are you talking about?'

'Don't do that,' she said with a shake of her head. 'Don't pretend like this is in my head. It isn't. I know what you're doing. I'm telling you what you're doing.'

'I wasn't doing that either.'

'No?' she asked. 'So being in control of your sister's relationship by *allowing* my brother to marry her, or telling us what to do after Liam left, or instructing me to follow you to speak with Emma, or now, when you took over a conversation I was having—you're saying none of that shows how you're controlling things?'

He opened his mouth to reply, but he started thinking about what she'd said and closed it again. He wasn't doing anything out of the ordinary. Taking charge, taking control was what he did. It was what he'd had to do since his father's death. It was what his siblings *needed* him to do. It had helped them all through unimaginable grief. So why was someone he'd just met making him feel guilty about it?

'Fine,' he said, his patience snapping. 'I'll do it alone. Because I don't run when things get hard. I take my responsibilities seriously and do what needs to be done.'

She hadn't been able to fall asleep, not until so late the sky had started lightening. When she'd woken up an hour later, she'd realised breakfast had started and she probably needed to be up. It would be a day of looking for her brother. And trying not to think about the night before.

Wonderful.

She took a quick shower, did her best with her make-up since her face gave away that she hadn't slept much. She didn't know what had kept her up. Was she anticipating a knock on the door? Either from Liam, coming to tell her he needed to talk, or from Caleb, coming to update her?

Or perhaps it was the concern that she'd overreacted at the dock? The persistent thought that she should apologise to Caleb and tell him *why* she'd overreacted? It was true that he was taking control. She was more sensitive to it than most. Every time something like that happened, her body stiffened. Since her muscles had been tight and achy almost the entire day, she knew she wasn't making it up.

But she didn't know if taking it out on him was

fair. A pesky voice in her brain insisted it wasn't, and pointed out all the good things he'd done the day before as proof. Things that told her he wasn't like the men in her past. That he didn't deserve to be painted with the same brush. At the same time, he still triggered that…that *fear* inside her. She didn't know the cause of it entirely, but it was as good a reason as any to make sure things between them remained cordial.

She resisted the involuntary snort.

Thirty minutes later, she was locking up and walking to breakfast. She didn't have to walk very far. Breakfast had been set up next to the pool in the centre of Pleasure Villas. One long table had a breakfast bar with food. Servers stood behind it, ready with spoons, a steady stream of others replacing empty containers. Another table had been set up as a coffee station. A short distance away from that, a long table decorated with fruits and flowers stood where people sat and ate.

Piper found Caleb almost immediately. Relief slid through her. Until that moment, she didn't realise how worried she was that he'd found something at the ticket stall last night and left without her. Not that she wanted to be involved with this mess. She was still planning on killing Liam when they found him. But he was still her brother. Plus, she was sure that if Caleb found him first, Liam's death wouldn't be as merciful as she intended on making it.

She didn't go to Caleb like she wanted to. Didn't demand any answers either. Instead, she headed for the coffee station, poured herself a cup, then leisurely made her way back to the table. She sat across from Caleb, Jada and Tate, the latter of whom were looking at her with a glower. It must run in the family. Caleb, however, watched her coolly. She returned the favour, bringing her cup to her lips.

She wasn't sure how long they sat like that, staring at one another. It was only when Jada released an irritated breath that Piper looked over.

'You're still upset with me,' she said.

'Yes.'

'Jada,' Caleb warned, but Piper waved a hand.

'It's fine. I get it.' She directed her attention to the younger Martin siblings. 'I'm sorry. I didn't know this would happen. There's no excuse for his behaviour.'

They blinked. Jada looked around. No one seemed to be interested in them. She turned back to Piper.

'It sucks.'

'It does.'

She looked deflated. 'I'm sorry we're taking this out on you. It's not your fault.'

Piper gave her a sympathetic smile. 'I understand.'

Jada and Tate exchanged a look, before both looking at Caleb. Something wordless passed between the three of them. Piper felt an inexplicable turn of jealousy in her stomach. No, not inexplicable—she knew the reason for it. She wished she could have had such a bond with her family. She would have settled for Liam, but she was still upset with him. Partly because he'd left her to deal with this. Another part was that she could see how upset Emma's family was. Knowing how upset Emma had been the day before, too, Piper was most upset that Liam had hurt Emma.

He was repeating their father's mistakes. Hurting the people he loved. Because, despite all this, Piper knew Liam loved Emma. But moving forward meant leaving the past behind. He'd managed some of that, untainted by their father, in the way his relationship with Emma had been before he'd run. If he wanted a future with her, he'd need to learn to stop running completely. She felt some responsibility for teaching him that. She might no longer have hope for herself to be unscathed by the past, but she did for Liam.

She looked up in surprise when Tate and Jada got up and, with murmured goodbyes, left.

'Did you chase them away?' she asked lightly, only then noticing that somehow they were alone at the end of the table. The closest guests were sitting four seats away.

'I didn't say anything to them.'

'Oh, you said something. Not verbally, but you told them something.'

Caleb's mouth pulled up at the side. 'You're perceptive.'

'When you're raised not to have a voice, you learn how to pay attention to what isn't said pretty well.'

Now his eyebrows pulled up. It took that for her to realise she'd said something revealing.

'Did you find anything last night?' she asked, changing the subject.

There was a moment of silence as he adjusted.

'You know,' he said slowly. 'One of these days, you're going to tell me what happened instead of alluding to it.' She barely had a chance to snort at the arrogance—or to register the thrill it brought—before he was continuing. 'And yes, I did. Liam bought a ticket to Santorini last night. He left on a ferry an hour before we caught up.'

'Santorini?' she repeated. 'What would he be doing there?'

'I don't know.' Caleb paused. 'I'd like to say he needs time to process, but he could do that here.'

'Except Liam likes to process away from the problem. As far away as he can get, actually.' She frowned. 'Santorini isn't that far, is it?' she asked. Caleb shook his head. 'Okay, so he intends on coming back.'

'You sound sure of that.'

'I'm not,' she said with a little laugh. 'But,

based on what I know…' She trailed off when she considered she didn't know that much. Not really. 'When Liam runs, it's clear when he's not coming back. If he wasn't planning on coming back now, he would have gone back to Cape Town. Probably,' she added, because she wasn't sure. 'Point is, there's a chance he'll be here for the wedding.'

'Do you want to take that chance?' he asked, his voice distant. 'There are only three days left.'

She frowned. 'It's not like we can go around Santorini trying to find him.'

'Why not? We did it here.'

'Because this island is small, and we knew what his steps were.'

'We know what his next step was. That's good enough for me.'

She exhaled, trying not to overreact again. *Cordial, Piper,* she reminded herself. With another breath, she nodded.

'I'm trying to help my sister,' he said after a moment. He'd been watching her. And he must have seen accusation on her face despite her attempt to school it if he was defending himself. 'I spent the entire night with her, waiting for her to wake up. When she did, I held her as she cried.' His jaw clenched. 'So—will you be coming with me?'

When she didn't answer immediately, he made a move to leave. Her hand shot out, startling both of them when it settled over the hand he had on the table. She ignored the heat of it, how it felt as if it were searing through her body from that small point of contact.

'Don't go,' she said softly. 'For one, you'll make a scene. You already have.' She smiled at him for the sake of the watching eyes, as if she were placating him somehow. 'The last thing Emma needs is for her guests to suspect something's wrong.'

His face settled into a blank expression—a smile was too much to ask for, apparently—but she could still see his anger in the way the corner of his mouth twitched.

Oh, why had she looked at his mouth? Despite the turmoil of feelings and tension happening inside and around her, that small gesture had her wondering what it would be like to kiss him. Would he be as demanding a kisser as he was as a man? Would his tongue ask her things and expect her to obey? Would she protest?

Startled by the intensity of her thoughts, she snatched her hand away. Midway through, she realised people were probably still watching and ran a hand down her ponytail instead. There was little chance of it looking natural, but at least she'd tried.

'What would you like them to think instead?' Caleb asked casually. He leaned back, watched her with interest.

It should have had alarms ringing in her head. It didn't. And it worried her. Worried her that she couldn't resist that look when she knew she should be able to.

'That we're having an argument?' he continued. 'Two lovers having a tiff?'

She fought to keep herself as calm as he appeared to be. 'We can be having an argument. I doubt anyone here would believe the nature of it to be romantic though.'

'Why not?'

'They're your friends and family,' she said simply. 'They know you.'

She left it at that, offering him a satisfied smile as she went to get herself some breakfast.

CHAPTER SIX

HE'D NEVER HAD these issues before. Perhaps he had been presumptuous, but he'd believed growing up with two sisters had taught him how to be around women. His history of successful dating stood testament to that. His interactions with Piper? Not so much.

The problem might have been that the dating didn't last too long. Sometimes, it carried on over weeks. A few months, in rare instances. But it always ended mutually, with each party satisfied.

Are you sure? Piper's voice asked in his head. He almost grunted, but then the real her—sitting across from him on the ferry, looking out the window—would have heard. She probably would have guessed he was talking to phantom Piper, too.

Yes, I am sure, he told that voice. *We both agreed things had gone as far as they could.*

Both of you? it asked. *Or did you simply make the decision* for *her, and she had no choice but to go along with you?*

He didn't answer that. It had nothing to do with the fact that a voice in his head had asked the question.

Most relationships aren't considered successful if they end, the voice spoke again.

Enough, he thought, clamping down on its freedom. Trying not to think about why he was having a conversation with himself in his head. Or why it felt as though he was having the conversation with the woman opposite him.

It felt like support for the fact that he'd never experienced this kind of animosity before. Animosity might have been too harsh a word, but what Piper radiated around him—and only him, he thought, remembering her interactions with his family—wasn't exactly positive.

He wondered what advice his father would have given him in the situation. Chad Martin never had problems speaking with people, no matter who they were. He could talk himself out of anything, and he'd been able to talk anyone *into* anything, too. When Caleb had taken over his father's business, he'd discovered he shared that with his father. It had connected them, had eased some of Caleb's grief as he worked to figure out how to be a property mogul in his late teens. Sometimes, Caleb wished he'd appreciated what he and his father had in common before Chad had died.

All of the time, he wished he'd just appreciated his father before Chad had died.

Caleb had been one of those annoying, sullen children. Fought his father at every opportunity. In Caleb's final year at school, Chad had urged him to get his real estate qualification. He'd refused, settling on studying towards a business degree for the sole purpose of annoying Chad. In the end, he'd followed his father's wishes—later, in his twenties, when he'd had a handle on being a businessperson and raising a family. Chad had handled the two roles easily. Caleb knew firsthand how hard it was, but Chad had never once shown it.

Maybe that was why Caleb felt the need to take care of everything for his siblings. To make sure they didn't have to worry, just like his father had once ensured for them. For *him*, Caleb corrected, something churning inside him. His siblings had been too young when Chad died to remember it.

'It'll be okay,' Piper said suddenly.

He frowned as his brain caught up to the present. She was staring at him, concerned.

'I'm sure it will be.'

'Are you?' she asked. 'You should tell that to your face.'

He grimaced, and she laughed. It was a happy sound, as if it had been hard fought for and was now finally free. The image made no sense and yet it made perfect sense. Which was yet another sign of what this woman was doing to his sanity.

'I wasn't thinking about this.'

'I'd like to ask you what you were thinking about, but I don't know if I should.'

'Me neither,' he agreed easily. 'You don't seem to like me much, so I doubt you'd want to know the inner workings of my mind.'

Her eyes went serious. He braced himself for a tongue-lashing.

'I don't know how I feel about you,' she said, in a tone similar to her expression. 'Despite that, I want to know what you were thinking about.'

It wasn't exactly a peace offering. Perhaps a temporary truce.

'I was thinking about my father,' he said, offering his own olive branch. 'I've been thinking about him a lot these days. It must be the wedding.'

'He passed away, right?'

'Yeah. Years ago—more than a decade.'

He looked out at the water splashing against the large windows of the ferry.

'But sometimes it still feels fresh?' she enquired gently.

He frowned, before remembering her father had passed away, too. 'It does. Do you feel that way?'

She blinked. Laughed without amusement. 'No.' The word was said curtly. 'Not about my dad. But I do sometimes feel that way about my mother. I think about how she'd react at big events in my life.' She chewed her bottom lip. 'I wonder about whether my life would be different if she hadn't died when we were so young.'

The unguardedness in her voice made him want to give her the same.

'I do that, too. Like now, I'm thinking about how he's missing out on all this. But maybe that's a good thing.' He shook his head as he said it. 'No, it's not. I don't know why I said that.'

'Because you feel it?' Her voice was soft. 'Maybe it's both a good *and* bad thing.' She shrugged at him. 'Human beings have complicated emotions. We don't always have to pick one thing over the other. We can let them be complicated, if they are.'

'Like your feelings for me?'

She stared at him, laughed with a shake of her head. 'I certainly have *strong* feelings about what I'd like to say to you now, yes.'

Caleb smiled, enjoying the lightness on her face. She was wearing her hair up again, with a cute summer dress and cute trainers. He wasn't sure if the cuteness came because that was what he found her to be, or if the items themselves were cute.

'Is this your first time in Greece?' he asked.

He wanted to know more about her. The sneak peek he'd got into her past now—that she missed her mother, but not her father—didn't seem to be enough. The strength of his desire to know surprised him.

'Yes.'

'The upside of Liam doing this then is that you'll get to see a little more of it.'

Her lips curved. Not enough for him to call it a smile, but enough to make his stomach ache with pleasure. He hadn't known that could happen until now.

'There are very few upsides to this, but I suppose that could be one, yes. Another,' she continued, 'is that we found out we'll be getting a new member of our family.'

He frowned. Somehow, he'd forgotten about that. Not entirely—it was likely somewhere at the back of his head. But with worrying about Emma and thinking about Piper, and trying *not* to think about Piper... No, he hadn't processed he was about to become an uncle.

He took a breath. 'Yeah, I guess we are.'

'What do you mean, you "guess"?' she asked, incredulous. 'Emma told us she was pregnant.'

'I'm...still struggling to believe it, I think.'

Piper studied him, then nodded slowly. 'Oh, I see. You're having trouble picturing your sister having sex.'

He reared back. He could feel his entire face crease in disgust. 'What is wrong with you?'

'Nothing's wrong with me. Sex is natural.'

Then—thankfully—she had mercy on him. 'Does this mean you're not happy about it?'

'Oh, it's not that. I've taken care of kids before. I can do it again if push comes to shove.' She gave him a look that made him realise how his words had sounded. 'I didn't mean—' He broke off, realising he *did* mean what he was about to say he didn't. 'I'm…worried, I suppose.'

'You shouldn't be.'

'The father of the baby ran off,' he said darkly. 'Why shouldn't I be?'

'He'll come back.'

'I thought you weren't confident about that.'

There was a moment before she answered. 'Fake it until you make it is a popular saying, I believe.' She sniffed.

He didn't know how or why it made him smile, but it did. Or how or why, when their gazes caught, he couldn't look away. Her eyes really were striking, her cheekbones so damn defined. He wanted to lift a hand and caress her cheek. Feel the skin that looked like satin, brush a thumb over her lips shortly after.

Speaking of…

He looked at those lips, saw them part under his perusal. It made him want to lean forward and kiss her. Slip his tongue through that parting and tease her until they forgot about their responsibilities—

Their responsibilities.

'I don't know if we can fake a groom on the wedding day,' he said gruffly, looking out of the window again. Wishing that the water could collapse over him and cool the tingling in his body.

'We won't have to.' Her voice was hoarse, too. It made him feel better. 'We'll find him, and I'll remind him of that.'

He looked at her now. 'Why does he need reminding?'

'How much do you know about my family, Caleb?' she asked seconds later.

'Not much more than you've told me,' he replied. 'Your parents passed away.'

She nodded. 'My dad only died five years ago, so he raised us.' She paused. 'He wasn't winning any Father of the Year awards. Most things in life we had to learn from books or TV. Things like responsibility.' Her fingers tightened in her lap. 'Liam is clearly still struggling with that.'

'How can he be? If your dad wasn't a good father, Liam must have looked out for you. That takes responsibility.'

She smiled at him. It reminded him of the day before, after he'd carried her, and she'd gone sad.

'I like that you think that,' she said softly. 'Almost enough to let you think all brothers look out for their younger siblings.'

He frowned. Thought about his sisters and brother. How lost they'd seemed after their father's death. How they'd needed love and protection. They'd needed *him,* and he'd given himself to them because he was their older brother. But young Piper apparently hadn't had that.

'Liam didn't look out for you.'

'No.' Her eyes flickered to him. 'It's not a reflection on his abilities to be a husband and a father.'

'Just a reflection on how poor a brother he is,' he said. 'Except you're still defending him.'

'Family is a hell of a thing,' she replied with a smile. 'Which is why you took care of your siblings after your father died. Why you still are.'

The way she said that last part niggled at him. He shrugged it off.

'My dad died when I was eighteen. Emma was the second oldest at eleven. It wasn't exactly a choice as much as a necessity.' He waited a beat. 'You know my mom left long before that.'

'I do. I'm sorry.'

'It is what it is.'

It was a facade of unaffectedness. Not so much about his mother—that part did make him feel rather unaffected. But his father's death at such a young age—how young his siblings had been when it happened—all of what his siblings hadn't got to experience because of it… Those were things that bothered him when he couldn't sleep. When his brain turned on and he couldn't switch it off again.

It happened more often than he wanted to

admit. He'd learnt to live with it, to cope with it, by working or working out. But sometimes his mind and his body were too tired for that. Not for the thoughts though. Or for the guilt.

Who in the universe had decided *he* should benefit from having his father around for eighteen years when his siblings hadn't?

'I remember,' Piper said, her eyes sharp when he looked at her, 'when I was around fifteen and Liam was seventeen, he was going through a… phase.'

'A phase?'

'He asked my father about it.'

'Wait—what exactly are we talking about here?'

'His body was changing.'

'At seventeen?' Caleb dropped his head, amusement shimmering through him. 'He was a late bloomer?'

She laughed, bright and sparkling like the water around them. 'Oh, I don't know. I think things might have already *bloomed* and he just wanted to do something about it then. He had a girlfriend. Carmen, I think. Or Camilla. I can never remember.'

He groaned. 'This is almost as bad as thinking about my sister having sex.'

'Which you shouldn't do.'

'Yeah, of course not.' He shifted in his seat. Stopped at the amusement on her face. She wanted him to squirm. He shouldn't enjoy it, but he did.

'Anyway, he asked my father about condoms or something and there was this moment of silence. You could hear a pin drop.' Her face went thoughtful. 'I wanted to laugh, but not because I found the moment funny. That's changed now, of course,' she told him. 'But then, it was because it was…awkward. Really, really awkward.'

His heart stalled at the look on her face. The way it had gone from teasing to something harder. More painful. More vulnerable.

'My father said, "no", and walked away.'

'He didn't answer the question.'

'No.' She met his eyes. 'It must have been hard for Liam to reach out to our father. But he was trying. I guess I'm trying with him now.'

'Hmm.' He took a few seconds before he continued. 'I hope he starts trying with you, too.'

She hadn't intended on telling him that story about her father. Or she had, but it wasn't meant to illustrate what a bad father hers had been. Or to imply that Liam needed to try and reach out to her. She'd only wanted to cheer Caleb up. Distract him from the obvious pain he felt about his own father.

But she couldn't stop thinking about it. Not even when they arrived in Santorini. At least not until something more pressing presented itself.

'I'm sorry—you want me to *what*?'

'Climb on the donkey,' Caleb said, as if it were a reasonable request. 'There are a lot of steps up to the village.'

'And riding a donkey up them is going to change that?'

'It'll make things a lot easier. We also get there quicker.'

'Except I'd be sacrificing my life in the process. Would speed and convenience make that worth it?' she asked him. 'Would you be happy if I died, but you got to the top of the island quickly and easily?'

'Do you always exaggerate this much?' he asked, narrowing his eyes. At least she assumed. He was wearing his sunglasses again. She didn't mind it as much now that she knew what was beneath it.

'I'm not exaggerating,' she told him. 'Look at that.'

She pointed at the area where the donkeys waited. They stared at her blandly. One flicked its tail, another stamped its hooves. The men waiting for them to decide muttered impatiently. Caleb sighed next to her.

'You're right. They're killing machines.'

'Why can't we stay here?' she asked, turning her back to the donkeys. 'It's gorgeous.'

The ocean twinkled in various shades of blue, the sun gleaming off it. It was midday, hot, though the sea breeze offered some relief. There were rocks in the distance, tall and rugged and brown. Boats navigated through them easily, stopped at the port regularly. There was chatter from tourists, from salespeople at the kiosks at the port, but it didn't change the beauty of the place.

'We can't stay here because these men say your brother went into the city.'

'They could be lying.'

'I offered them enough incentive to be truthful,' he said dryly.

'Doesn't mean they're telling the truth. If you were offering me money to ask if I'd seen some guy, I'd do exactly what they did.'

'No, you wouldn't.'

'No, I wouldn't.' Should it bother her that he knew that about her? 'I'm still not getting on that donkey. Not even if you pay me for it.'

She walked past the animals, barely sparing a glance for them, though her heart beat painfully in her chest. She'd had one experience with donkeys on a school trip when she was twelve. She'd been scarred by it. She still remembered how they rode in a circle in an enclosed track. The donkey had gone faster than it was supposed to, spooked by something no one had been able to disclose to her. At no point had she been unsafe, but she'd learnt her lesson about the unpredictability of the animal. She couldn't imagine what would happen if a donkey got unpredictable on a flight of steps.

By the tenth step, she knew she would pay for this decision. By the twentieth, she was breathing hard, and she was barely a quarter of the way up. At the thirty-fifth she stopped, put her hands on her waist and panted.

'Regretting this decision now?'

She whirled around. When the movement made her unsteady, she pressed her back against the mountain. It was cooler there, and she closed her eyes on an exhale. When she opened her eyes again, Caleb was still there, watching her, as un-ruffled as ever.

'I didn't realise you were climbing with me,' she said, her voice breathy.

'Did you think I'd climb on a donkey and wait for you at the top?' he asked sarcastically. She almost made a sarcastic reply in return before she realised it would take energy she didn't have. Which annoyed her because not only was he not breathing hard, but he had the energy to be sar-castic with her, too.

'I would have been able to suffer in silence then,' she breathed, closing her eyes again.

'Your wish is my command.'

After a moment, she wished he hadn't listened to her. Or that she'd said something about him watching her as well. Though she couldn't see him do it, she could feel him. She opened her eyes, caught him. Then found herself caught, just as she had been on the boat.

He'd taken off his sunglasses, giving her direct access to his gaze. It was…intense. Being its focus made her feel as if she wanted to curl up in front of him, purr. She didn't get the chance to be embarrassed by the thought when emotion flickered across his face.

'What?' she asked, pulling her ponytail over her shoulder when it made her feel self-conscious.

'I was going to ask you the same thing,' he replied. 'What were you thinking about now?'

'I…wasn't… I mean, I…'

'Piper,' he said when she stopped stammering. When she gave up on trying to form a full sentence. 'You're charming when you're embarrassed. Has anyone ever told you that before?'

Her cheeks flushed, but she shook her head. A donkey rattled past them, then two more. Caleb moved closer to her to get out of the way. It brought him very much into *her* way. She lifted her chin to meet his eyes, though heaven only knew why she would. She shouldn't look at him when this…this strange *thing* was happening between them. When she still wanted to purr, but now, with his body centimetres away from her, wanted him to pet her, too.

Stroke a hand down the curve of her spine… have his hand settle on her lower back… He'd pull her even closer, until there was no space between them. Lower his lips to hers, so she could taste that contrary mouth of his. She would feel what she knew would be a hard, firm body against her softness. She might even be tempted into hooking a leg around his waist so that—

Her mouth opened and she drew in air. She couldn't breathe, and it had nothing to do with her climbing up the steep steps to the village of Oia. It was because she'd just thought about Caleb *petting* her. Her brother's future brother-in-law. A man she would share a family member with when Emma gave birth. Not only that—though the entire idea of being petted spoke wonders about her sanity—it had nothing to do with petting at all. She wanted to make out with him. To taste him and feel him. To indulge that faint buzz inside her that told her their connection wasn't only physical attraction. To pretend that was the most important thing she had to do.

But it wasn't. She had to think. Her brain had helped her survive the years of her father's control. Obeying him had been better than the alternative: fights and punishments, the latter getting crueller as she grew older.

He'd be late on payment for school fees, so she'd have to take a letter home or not get her report card when everyone else did. He wouldn't fetch her after school, or he'd make her wait. He wouldn't help her apply for university. He certainly didn't help apply for funding.

But she'd survived it—only to find someone else who'd treated her exactly the same.

She couldn't make those same mistakes now. Oh, Caleb might seem different, but what if he wasn't? What if he *allowed* her to do things? Or took over, and made her think she couldn't do things herself?

It had happened before. It could happen again.

She couldn't be wooed by this man. She had to break through whatever spell he'd woven over her...

'They're done,' she said quietly. Dipped her head. No more eye contact. 'I'm ready to climb again.'

She did exactly that, not stopping again even when her lungs started to burn and her legs felt sore and heavy. They were halfway now, then three-quarters of the way up. Still, she didn't stop. Her legs were burning now, too. There was a stitch in her side.

Good, she thought. She'd punish herself for whatever had happened with them at that step. It would be a reminder that she shouldn't have been in that position. She should have been protecting herself. She couldn't entertain the idea of a make-out session with this man. It would no doubt bring her the emotional equivalent of the physical pain she was currently feeling.

'Piper,' came a voice from beside her. It was joined by a gentle but firm grasp around her arm. She refused the pleasure of its warmth. Pulled away.

'What?'

'You're pushing yourself too hard.'

'I'm…climbing,' she said between huffs. Now that she was standing still, her body was berating her for doing exactly as Caleb said.

'Yeah, but you're not taking breaks.'

'Neither…are you.'

'I don't need them.'

'Oh, right,' she said, rolling her eyes. 'Because…you're a perfect…male specimen.'

The biting tone of the words was undermined by the breathiness.

'I'm only saying if you need a break, take one.'

She narrowed her eyes at him. He grunted. Then made another sound that was strangled.

'How about if I go ahead? Would you feel more comfortable with stopping, going at your own pace then?'

No.

'Yes,' she replied, out of spite.

His eyes swept over her face. He gave her a curt nod.

'I'll wait for you at the top.'

He began to climb the steps, and her gaze immediately dipped to the muscular calves, the strong legs, the fine butt. There was that spell again, she thought. It pointed out how rude she was being when he'd been perfectly kind to her, despite how inconvenient she'd made this climb for him.

But perhaps this was good. Perhaps he should be annoyed with her. Angry, even. That way, he wouldn't be tempted to give into that pull she knew he felt, too. If he didn't, it would give her another layer of protection. He didn't pursue her; she didn't fall for him. Easy.

Her eyes found him climbing the steps again, admired him within seconds.

Hmm. Not so easy, then.

CHAPTER SEVEN

HE WAS GOING to get a crick in his neck from turning around so often. Not that it mattered, since he'd probably die from falling down the steep steps he was climbing first. It wasn't a good idea to keep checking on Piper. He needed to focus, to climb, to get to the top of this damn island. But the arguments were useless. The fact that he turned once again, looked for her frame, proved it.

She gave him a headache. Everything about her was annoying, contrary, and so *appealing*. He wanted to know why him taking charge bothered her so much. Why she had such a problem with his suggestions. He wanted to know why there was that moment after he'd make a suggestion. She'd blink, tilt her head slightly, then look directly into his eyes and give him an answer. Her brain was obviously working, and he wanted to know what it was doing.

But she infuriated him almost as much as she intrigued him. The more it happened, the more it irritated him. He was trying to help her. Especially since it seemed she wouldn't help herself.

When he'd pointed out that she was pushing herself, she'd seemed surprised. He couldn't tell if that surprise was because she hadn't noticed, or because he had. Surely the latter. She must have known she was pushing herself too hard. Her face was pink, her breathing laboured. He'd wanted to stop her earlier, but thought she would herself, as she had the first time. It was only when he'd heard her gasp for air—a literal gasp—that he'd intervened.

He didn't think she'd noticed she'd done it.

It was tempting to take up the offer of one of the waiters peering out of their restaurants. Cold drinks, a meal? It sounded like heaven. But it would waste unnecessary time. He needed to remember why he'd come here, which was to find his sister's fiancé. He couldn't go into a restaurant, enjoy a cold beer when—

Wait. There was something there.

He stopped, getting what he imagined was a curse word from the man behind him. It was in a foreign language, one he didn't recognise, but he knew it nevertheless. He'd used the same tone countless times before. In fact, because of it, he turned back and apologised, before asking the nearest waitress if she could speak English.

'Of course,' she said without skipping a beat. 'Would you like a table, sir? For how many? One? Two?'

'Neither. I was hoping you could help me with something.'

Her face changed. Another thing he'd seen many times before, particularly from people who were propositioned regularly. Her expression became guarded. Her eyes hooded. To her credit, or perhaps to the shame of the tourists who'd flirted with her, her smile didn't fade.

'How can I help?'

'I'm looking for a man.'

Her brow furrowed. 'A man?'

'Yes. He's about my height, brown hair, brown skin. I think brown eyes.'

'Sir, you are describing many people.'

'Sure,' he said. He looked down, wondering how far behind Piper was. She had a photo of Liam on her phone, which would probably be quite useful.

She was still climbing, giving way to a few tourists who were pushing behind her. She looked frazzled, her face no less pink than earlier, her breathing no less laboured. He thought her beautiful. Breathtaking, actually, since he was struggling to get air into his lungs watching her.

'Sir?' When he turned, the waitress was regarding him with amusement. The traces of hostility on her face had disappeared. 'Your wife is very beautiful.'

'My… That woman over there?' he asked. Unnecessarily, since they both knew who she was talking about. 'She's not my wife.'

'Oh,' the waitress replied, disappointed. 'I am sorry. Your girlfriend? Fiancée?'

'We're not in a relationship.'

'But—' She cut herself off with a knowing smile. 'Ah, you pine. Do not worry,' she said, patting his arm. 'If it is meant to be, it will be.'

He didn't comment on that, too offended by her assumption to even—

Oh, who was he kidding? There was absolutely a part of him that pined—in a way he never had before. The annoyance, the frustration were merely excuses not to face it. Facing it would be a distraction. He had proof of that, didn't he? He'd already considered abandoning his search for Liam the night before because of her. But he couldn't. He needed to do this for Emma. His father would have wanted him to.

A familiar weight settled on his shoulders. They ached at the strain, but reminded him the weight hadn't *settled*. That implied it had gone, even for a moment. It hadn't. It never did. It was simply heavier now. More acute because Emma needed him and he was afraid of letting her down.

That fear was almost crippling. It made him

think terrible things. Things that made him feel even guiltier than usual. Like how he wished, for once, his siblings could take care of themselves. That he could be free of the weight— of it all.

He shook his head. The fear wouldn't cripple him. And he wouldn't indulge such terrible thoughts. His family needed him. There would be no pining. No distractions. There was only finding Liam.

'Waiting for me?' Piper asked from the step below him.

'Yes.' His voice was curt. He had to stop himself from telling her it wasn't about her when he caught the quick flash of hurt on her face before she hid it. 'I'm not doing a good job of explaining how Liam looks.'

Piper looked at the waitress. 'Did he tell you the man had brown hair and brown skin?'

The woman smirked. 'Yes.'

Piper shook her head. 'How did you describe him to whoever was at the ticket stall last night?'

'Exactly like that. The man found it sufficient.'

'Ah, the man.' Piper looked at the waitress again, digging out her phone from her bag. 'See how he's implying the ability to describe someone is gendered?' She shook her head. 'Men.'

The waitress laughed, looked him straight in the eye and smiled. 'I see why you pine, sir. She is marvellous.'

* * *

Oh, that uncomfortable comment had been worth the look on Caleb's face.

She was still trying to figure out why the waitress had said it an hour later. Not that she should have been thinking about that. The woman hadn't seen Liam, nor had the other waiters from the restaurants on the steps to Oia. They hadn't had much luck with the shops in the immediate vicinity either.

Now they were both exhausted, hungry, with no clear route to follow.

'Do we give up?' Piper asked, leaning against the railing on top of a wall that stood between restaurants. She imagined it was to keep people from falling over, although she couldn't imagine anyone doing so.

Then again, the view *was* spectacular enough for accidents to happen.

The endless stretch of sea was idyllic in its vastness, a reminder of how tiny human beings truly were. Oia was known for its sunsets, and Piper could only imagine what an experience that must be. Seeing the light go from yellow to orange to pink in the blue sky. Watching the sun disappear behind the dark blue ocean. She nearly sighed at the picture it made in her imagination. Badly wanted to be able to look at it in reality.

'We can't give up,' Caleb said from beside her. He was watching her, not the view. She was suddenly reminded of the waitress's words, and felt her face flush.

'What do we do next, then?' she asked, looking back at the ocean. 'We have no leads. We can't keep going around asking people if they've seen Liam.'

'We can. We should.'

'Caleb,' she said on a sigh, 'that idea is impractical. There are too many pathways, too many shops, too many people here. The chances of us—'

'We have to try,' he interrupted. 'I can't go back to Emma without news.'

'What if he's already gone?' she asked, intrigued by his intense reaction.

'Where would he go? He'd have to take a bus to the airport or ferry… We should go to the bus station,' Caleb said, straightening. 'Or go back down to the port. Ask them if Liam came back. We didn't think about that, Piper. We should have thought about that.'

'Caleb,' she said again. This time she put a hand on his arm. Unsurprisingly, the swell of his biceps was firm and large beneath her fingers. 'You sound like you're spiralling.' At his blank expression, she elaborated. 'Out of control.'

'What?' he asked, head jerking back. 'No. I'm in control. I'm always in control.'

For some reason, the statement didn't repel her as it should have. Again, she worried about it, but the feeling was overwhelmed by a different worry. Not for her missing brother or the wedding he was running from. But for Caleb. He seemed… untethered. He must have felt it, too, which clearly bothered him.

She tried not to think about why she cared. Why a man losing control, when other men had exerted it over her, affected her so much.

'Okay, you're in control.' She dropped her hand. It might make him feel more comfortable. 'How about we take a moment to think things through? We'll get some lunch, something cool to drink. Think about our strategy.'

He protested—of course he protested—but eventually she wore him down. They walked to the closest restaurant, checked out the menu. Piper winced as she did the currency conversion in her head, thinking that a single meal cost as much as an entire day's food back home.

She'd always been careful with money. For one, because she'd rarely had any growing up. Because of that, she recognised it as the commodity it was. Recognised all the things it could bring her.

Perhaps that was why she'd fallen for Brad. He'd come from money. It was never an issue for him, so he swept her up and away and she could have whatever the hell she liked. Except it hadn't been the freedom she'd thought it was. Certainly not with him. Each expensive meal, each expensive gift, had come at a cost. A party she couldn't attend. A dinner she had to go to. After that she'd realised it wasn't money that was the commodity; it was having her own. Not depending on anyone else.

She'd started working long before that realisation had settled, despite her father's protests. It was her first real—and only—act of rebellion. It had come at sixteen, after Liam had left for university. It had barely been legal to work then, but it had taken her out of the house. She'd had to give half of her salary to her father, but she'd saved the rest. Used it to buy textbooks for her degree in education when her funding didn't cover it and her father had refused to help.

He'd died before she'd started dating Brad, a man who'd wanted to spend money on her. But, just as her father had kept money from her to control her, Brad had spent money on her to control her. When she'd broken up with him, he'd taken back everything he'd given her. She saw it as a lesson, and appreciated it. Now, she bought what she wanted when she wanted to, and all for herself.

That didn't mean she could justify spending an entire day's budget on one meal. Especially since she'd already had the unexpected cost of the ferry.

'We don't have to eat here.'

'What?' she asked, blinked back into the present. 'Oh, no, it's fine. I was just…thinking about what I'd be eating back home.'

'What?'

'A chicken sandwich.'

'A chicken sandwich,' he repeated. Shook his head. 'You are not having a chicken sandwich in Greece, Piper. Come on.'

He walked towards a different restaurant, one he seemed to know, before stopping and coming back to where she stood. She hadn't moved to follow him.

'I'm sorry. That was a bit…bulldozing of me.' He frowned at the words, as if he couldn't believe they'd come from his mouth. 'I'd like to take you to a restaurant I've been to before. It has some authentic Greek food I would love for you to try.' He paused. 'If you'd like to come.'

Her lips twitched. He was frowning too deeply to notice.

She schooled her face. 'What if I don't?'

He opened his mouth, closed it. The frown got deeper, though she had no idea how that was possible. 'We can go somewhere that'll give you a damn chicken sandwich.'

'Together?' she asked, her voice more delighted than she'd given permission for it to be. 'Would you really?'

'If that's what you want.' He looked at her, expression pained, then it cleared. 'You're pulling my leg.'

'I was. But now I kind of want to go to some place that'll give you a chicken sandwich to see if you'd go through with it.'

'Isn't my admission enough?'

She tilted her head, felt warmth spread through her. 'Yeah, it is. Come on, let's go.'

He grinned, and the warmth that had initially been innocent turned into something dangerously lusty.

'Thanks. You'll love this place. It gets great reviews. I went with a friend years back when I first came to Greece and we ate like kings.'

'Sounds expensive.' She hated saying it. Hated how small her voice sounded.

'Yeah, but it's worth—' He broke off. 'Yes, it is. I'm sorry.'

'Why are you apologising?'

'It was presumptuous of me.'

She stiffened. 'I can pay for expensive meals if I want to.'

'Of course,' he said with a frown. 'I was talking about how it's presumptuous of me to assume you'd let me pay. It's not a date or anything,' he clarified quickly. 'It's the least I can do, with everything you've done for Emma. She told me how kind you've been to her. That helped her with the plans for the wedding.'

'I didn't,' she said, shaking her head.

'You made the gifts, didn't you?'

'Yes, but they're stupid little crafts. Flowers.'
She shrugged. 'Nothing to write home about.'

'Except it made her happy. She was so pleased
you were contributing.' He waited. 'Will you let
me pay for lunch?'

'Like you've paid for the accommodation? And
the flights? And all the meals while we're here?'

'That was for all the wedding guests, not only
you.'

She studied him, then rolled her eyes. 'Fine.
But just this once.'

He grinned again. *Oh,* her insides sighed.

She was going to have to figure out some kind
of protection against the potency of it.

'You've made me a happy man, Piper.'

'Must be all that pining,' she replied easily,
smiling at the mortification on his face.

CHAPTER EIGHT

'Wow, this is...'

Piper didn't finish her sentence, only stared out of the window next to the table they'd been seated at. He loved watching her take in the Greek experience. Her joy and astonishment were genuine. There was a purity in it that reminded him his travels had desensitised him to beauty.

No, he thought immediately, eyes flickering over Piper's face. He could still appreciate beauty. He supposed it depended on the form it came in then.

'You should see it at sunset,' he told her, thanking the waiter as the man filled their glasses with water. 'It's one of the best views in the city.'

'I can imagine,' she said, eyes big. Pure.

'I'll show you some time.'

She didn't speak, only gave him a small smile that reminded him she wouldn't be there long enough for him to show her. Suddenly he wanted nothing more than to ask her to stay. He'd take some more time off work—hell, he'd been working non-stop for the last thirteen years; a month wouldn't matter—and he'd show her the world.

He'd start with Greece, with sunsets in Oia, then he'd take her on a boat trip to visit all the islands. They'd fly to Italy—to Venice, where he'd take her on a gondola ride and watch her as she was serenaded. They'd go to Scotland so she could appreciate the countryside; to Bora Bora so she could relax in the sun.

And all the while he would enjoy her. Enjoy experiencing these countries he'd gone to before but never appreciated, through her eyes.

The intensity of his fantasy startled him. No, not the fantasy: the emotion accompanying it. The deep desire. The *yes, please* his heart sighed at the prospect.

Maybe he was losing his mind. Perhaps he *had* fallen down the steps when he'd been checking for her earlier. This was a dream he was having while unconscious—or possibly dead. But when Piper looked out of the window again, her eyes softening, appreciation lighting up her entire face, he knew he couldn't be dead. If he was, he was in heaven. Considering how ungrateful he'd been before his father's death, he wasn't sure he'd end up in heaven. At least not until he balanced the scales. Until he made his father proud by being the kind of family man Chad had been.

Why did that feel like more of a hardship when he was with Piper?

'What are you thinking about?' she asked him, her eyes no longer on the view but on him.

For how long? What had she seen?

'You ask me that a lot.'

'If I recall, you've asked me the same thing,' she retorted. Quirked a brow. 'So, are you going to tell me?'

He considered for a short moment. 'I was thinking that I'd like to show you the sunset.'

'Oh.' Colour lightly stained her cheeks. She frowned. 'You were upset by that?'

'The prospect didn't…not please me.'

'Your expression showed more than a lack of pleasure.' She cocked her head. 'Then again, you have resting annoyed face, so perhaps I'm reading too much into this.'

'Resting annoyed face?' he asked, amused. 'That's a thing?'

'With you it is.'

'Yours isn't much better.'

She fluttered her lashes. 'Are you sure? I've been told I have resting sunshine face.'

'By whom?'

'My students. Their parents.'

'You're a teacher?'

'Yes,' she said, the teasing tone leaving her voice. 'You didn't know?'

'How would I have known that?'

'You didn't do research? Make sure you knew the family your sister was marrying into?'

'I…'

He hesitated, embarrassed that he had. That, in fact, he did know she was a teacher; he just hadn't remembered. It was different when the information he'd read was abstract. Liam had a younger sister. She was a teacher. But now that he knew Piper, knew it was her the information was describing… Part of him wished he could go back and read it again. But that didn't help him now.

'So you did know,' Piper said with a curve of her lips that wasn't a smile. 'Why am I not surprised?'

'I was looking out for Emma.'

'Of course,' she said smoothly. 'What else did you find out?'

'Only what you've already told me about your parents.'

'I don't suppose the research told you I miss the idea of my mother more than I do the memory of her?'

A trap, he thought. He didn't reply.

'Or that I don't miss my father at all?' Her eyes went cold. 'I'm only sorry he didn't die sooner.'

Silence followed. A horrifying, awkward, stunned silence. Out of the corner of Caleb's eye, he saw the waiter walk towards them, take in the scene, pause, then turn to another table, pretending they'd called him. Caleb couldn't blame the man. He didn't understand why he wanted to comfort Piper instead of fleeing then. He wanted to pull her in his arms, soothe her until the ice in her eyes defrosted and the shame permeating off her as her skin turned red subsided.

She let out a harsh breath.

'I'm sorry. That was...' She trailed off. Looked at him. 'Uncomfortable, wasn't it?'

'I'm sorry you feel that way.' He was sorrier that his actions had prompted her to rehash it. 'I didn't mean to pry. I only wanted Emma to be safe.'

'What did you think you'd find?' she asked, going for light-heartedness, he thought, but not quite succeeding. 'Links to a prominent South African gang?'

'Maybe.' Wanting to give her some relief from it, he said, 'I was disappointed to find nothing scandalous, I admit.'

She smiled. It went from relieved to curious in seconds.

'You're protective of them, aren't you?' she asked. 'Emma and Jada and Tate?'

'Unreasonably so.'

'Why?'

'Why?' he repeated with a small smile. 'They're my siblings. My younger siblings. Whom I raised.'

'Ah. *That's* why you feel protective of them.'

'I think generally siblings are protective of one another.'

'So they're protective of you, too?'

He frowned. 'I… I don't know.'

'That makes me feel better about my relationship with Liam,' she commented after a brief pause.

'You're looking for him now. That must come from being protective.'

'I suppose,' she said thoughtfully. 'Maybe he just isn't protective of me.' She laughed, but it was strangled.

'He seemed protective when he called me at the airport yesterday,' he pointed out. 'He sounded worried.'

Something passed over her face. A mixture of hope and resignation.

'I don't know what to tell you,' she replied. 'We had a hard childhood. As soon as Liam could leave, he left. Except he left me alone with that hardness. We really only reconnected after my dad died. More so when Emma came into the picture.' She smiled. 'She definitely had something to do with that. I think she shares your view on siblings.'

It should have soothed the unsettledness her question about how his siblings felt about him had evoked. It didn't.

'Maybe you do, too. You're here,' he said again. 'You obviously care about him.'

'That's part of the problem.' Her smile turned sad. 'I can't seem to stop caring about him.

There's a…loyalty I feel for him that he doesn't feel for me.'

'He loves you.'

'What does love mean if there's no action?' she asked. With a quick shimmy of her shoulders and a now shaky smile, she reached for her menu. 'I should probably get something more interesting than water to drink.'

She perused the list, giving it more attention than selecting a drink deserved. He understood. There was a part of him that was tempted into doing the same. Finding something trivial to distract him. But he couldn't. Her words kept echoing in his head.

What does love mean if there's no action?

She was right. Love was *doing* something, not merely saying it. He knew it because his mother had told him she loved him, but she'd still left.

Susan Martin had been a present mother for the first twelve years of Caleb's life. She'd got pregnant in university, dropped out to take care of him while his father built his business, and then went back three years later to get her degree. It had taken her longer than most, but she'd graduated. She must have still been happy at that point because they'd decided to have another child…and another…and another. He suspected his youngest brother and sister weren't as planned as Emma had been. Suspected it because his mother had left when Tate was one, claiming her life had got away from her.

He'd been twelve when she'd told him that. He remembered the day clearly. There had been shouting in the living room between her and his father. Tears when she'd come into the room, kissed his siblings goodnight, stopped with him. She'd leaned in, said those words, apologised, then told him she loved him. He hadn't believed her.

He wasn't angry that she didn't care for the demands of being a mother or wife. He believed that she had the right to do whatever she wanted. She could find her value in contributing to a family or to a company. In doing both. Neither. Honestly, he didn't care. What he did care about was *when* she'd figured that out. After she'd already been married for twelve years, with four children, three of them aged five or younger.

His mother had been the perfect example of how love didn't matter without action. Which was why he'd acted after his father's death. Part of it had been to make up for being a terrible teenager, yes. But a bigger part was to live up to his father's legacy. To give his siblings the space to make mistakes and learn, like his father had done for him. Like his father would have done for them if he hadn't died.

But when does it stop?

A piercing sound prevented him from pondering the disturbing thought. Piper dug into the handbag that had been hanging over her chair. When she saw the display, she looked at him with wide eyes.

'It's Liam.'

'Let me talk to him,' Caleb said immediately.

'No,' Piper said, disappointment coursing through her. *Protect yourself,* it seemed to say, highlighting how commanding Caleb's tone had sounded. *Stop falling for him. It'll only lead to heartache.*

She took a steadying breath. 'If he wanted to talk to you, he would have called you.'

Caleb swore. She ignored him.

'Hello?'

'Pie?' Liam said.

'Yeah, of course. Who else would it be?'

'You could have given your phone to one of the Martins.'

'Why would I do that?'

'You wouldn't. Of course you wouldn't.'

Liam sounded relieved. As if he'd really worried one of the Martins would be listening in on the conversation.

Well, that was half true. But Liam didn't have to know that.

'Where are you?'

'In Santorini.'

'Santorini?' Piper repeated, straightening. 'You're still here?'

'What do you mean, still? And here?'

'I…er…' She pulled her face at Caleb, who was watching attentively. He made a *go on* gesture with his hands. Easy for him to say. 'I meant you're still here in Greece. We were sure you'd left.'

'We?' he asked. 'So you are working with the Martins?'

'I've been forced into co-operating with them since I'm your only relative at this wedding. They were wondering why you'd run away from a woman you clearly care about. They thought I'd have answers. Heaven only knows why.'

'I'm sorry,' he said. To his credit, he sounded sincere. 'I…panicked. I needed some time to breathe.'

'You couldn't have chosen some other time? Maybe some other place, too? Like back home, not four days before your wedding in a different country?'

'There's some new information——' He broke off, released a huff of air. 'Look, I called for a favour. I need you to stall.'

'I will not.'

'Pie, please. I can't come back, and I'm surprised Caleb hasn't hired a private investigator to find me.'

'Yet,' she said darkly.

'Exactly. Buy me some time. Tell them I'm safe in Santorini. I need a moment to get my head right.'

'How long is that moment going to be?'

'Not long,' he promised. 'I'll be back for the wedding.'

'Yeah?' she asked, not believing him. 'So you want me to tell your fiancée that you need time but you'll be back for the wedding?'

'Please.'

'Liam, you're being ridiculous.'

'You don't understand—'

'So make me. Where are you staying?'

'What?'

'I'll come to the island and we can have a conversation about what you're going through. That's the only way I'll stall for you.' She met Caleb's eyes. He was fuming, but he didn't say anything.

At least he exerted control over himself, too.

After a moment of hesitation, Liam named a hotel.

'I'll see you in an hour.'

'What?' he said, surprise in his voice. 'It isn't going to take an hour for you to get to Santorini from Mykonos.'

'As luck would have it,' she said dryly, 'I'm already on my way. Good thing I thought today would be a good day for exploring Greece.'

CHAPTER NINE

'LET'S GO,' SAID Caleb as soon as she put down the phone.

'If I show up there now, he'll think I was lying to him.'

'You are lying to him,' Caleb pointed out. 'I'm also wondering why you said *I,* as if you're the only one going to meet him.'

'I am.'

'Really?' Caleb said casually. Dangerously. 'We're not in this together then, are we?'

'Of course we are,' she replied a little irritably.

Although she was more irritated at herself. She would have been annoyed if he'd assumed she wouldn't go with him if the roles were reversed. But she didn't like that he'd assumed. Didn't like that it felt as if she was giving in when, logically, she knew she wasn't.

Oh, her father and Brad had messed up her brain. Given her complexes. Complicated the way she interacted with people. With men. Even those who seemed safe.

Safe?

'Explain to me how this is going to work?' Caleb asked before she could explore where that word had come from.

'You'll go with me to the hotel. Stay out of sight while I try to talk some sense into Liam.' She was tired of the tension now. 'Once I do, you're free to make yourself known. Just don't scare him off.'

'If he's that easily scared, he doesn't deserve Emma.'

'Yes,' she agreed. 'But she still wants him, which is more important, isn't it?' She lifted a hand, calling for the waiter. 'Now, I figure we have about thirty minutes before we have to wrap things up here. Why don't we order something that'll sate our stomachs, then get going?'

He studied her, then picked up his menu, asked her opinion on some options that would be quick. By the time the waiter arrived, they'd selected three appetisers to share, including at least two different forms of carbs. Piper ordered an iced tea to go with it, though a glass of wine would have gone down smoother. Anything, really, with alcohol in it. But she needed her wits about her, and drowning her sorrows in wine had never got her anywhere.

Unfortunately.

'Look,' Caleb said when the waiter left, 'I don't mean to come across as though I'm…taking control.' He said the phrase with such distaste she had to hide her smile. 'But I need to make sure this goes right for Emma.'

'Okay.'

'Okay?' he asked, blinking. 'I thought you were going to give me a tongue-lashing for sure.'

'The fact that you know that means I don't need to.' Which was interesting. Was that why she suddenly thought him *safe*? 'Anyway, I'm too tired to fight. We've already argued today and—' she leaned forward '—my legs are *aching*. Did you know there are over a hundred steps up to this city? *A hundred.* I stopped counting after that and we were barely past halfway.'

He chuckled. 'They should look into building a lift.'

She regarded him carefully. 'You're a millionaire, aren't you? *You* should look into that.'

His laugh was louder, bolder now. Full of life and happiness. It bloomed inside her like flowers in the spring. Made her feel fresh and new in a way she hadn't experienced before.

He was trouble, she thought. The more time she spent with him, the deeper she fell into the trouble. She could tell not only by the fact that her body liked his, but that her mind liked his. And that they could go from squabbling and annoying one another to making one another laugh within minutes.

She thought back to how considerate he'd been with her when she'd been prickly on the steps.

How he apologised for making assumptions. How he seemed to have taken her accusation of him taking control and engaged with it. Apologised for it. How he was adapting to it. How he was protective of his siblings. How outraged he'd been on her behalf when she'd told him Liam wasn't protective of her.

She liked all of it. She liked…she liked him.

Oh, he was *definitely* trouble.

'He's gone,' Piper said when she came out of the hotel.

At first, Caleb thought he'd heard wrong. Liam couldn't be *gone*.

'What do you mean?' he asked. 'Are we meant to meet him somewhere else?'

She gave him a strange look. 'No. The man at reception told me I missed him. By minutes, apparently.'

'Piper,' he said after a moment, 'are you telling me that if we'd got here earlier, we might have seen Liam?'

She lifted her chin. 'Maybe. But he left a note to say he'd like to meet me here tomorrow instead.' She showed him the note, which had the name of a restaurant on the opposite side of the island. 'He wants to meet at lunchtime.'

'Because he's clearly demonstrated how well he keeps his appointments,' Caleb said sarcastically. 'This is terrible.'

'It's not,' she said. 'We know where he'll be.'

'If he shows up.'

'He will.'

'Really? You're defending him.'

'Absolutely not. But he had the decency to leave a note. He made another appointment. I'm going to give him the benefit of the doubt. Maybe he needed more time, like he said.'

'This is the definition of defending him.'

'Yeah, well, we've already established I'm a fool.'

She gave him a smile that broke his heart. Damn it, he couldn't be angry any more.

'I'm sorry he disappointed you.'

'I'm sorry he's disappointing Emma.'

'Emma.' Caleb groaned. 'She asked me to call her with an update.'

'So call her and tell her what we know.'

'Which is what?'

'We're seeing him tomorrow.'

'How am I supposed to explain that he'll be gone from her another day?'

'You don't have to, Caleb,' she said gently. 'He will, when they see one another again.' She reached out, squeezed his forearm. 'I'll give you some privacy.'

He watched as she walked up the narrow path to the top of the island. Her legs were beautiful, toned, almost golden. They were also entirely inappropriate to look at when he was supposed to be calling his sister with bad news.

With a twisted stomach, he called Emma. He kept the conversation short, trying hard not to feel guilty when she quietly started crying. He did end up feeling like a coward though, when he said goodbye at the first possible moment. When he joined Piper again, he thought he had the emotion of it under control. One look told him he hadn't succeeded.

'That bad, huh?'

'She was crying,' he said. 'I think that qualifies as being bad.'

'It does.'

She reached out, squeezed his arm again. He was getting used to it as a show of comfort. The action, not the explosion of warmth that went through his body every time she touched him.

'There isn't anything I can do about it except hope that he shows tomorrow.' Caleb sighed. Then realised they needed to make plans. 'What are we going to do?'

'What do you mean?'

'Are we going to wait here? Go back to Mykonos?'

'That's over seven hours of travelling in two days.' She sighed. 'I suppose we'll have to.'

'Or we could stay here.'

'How?'

'I have a place on the other end of the island.

Close to where Liam wants to meet, actually.'
He wondered why he was so nervous making the
offer. 'We could watch the sunset here, get a car
and stay over there for the night.'

'It wouldn't be…imposing?'

'Not at all. I usually hire out the place during
the peak season but, with Em's wedding, I thought
we might need it.'

'Always prepared, aren't you?'

He smiled. 'I try to be.'

'What are the chances you prepared for this,
though?' she asked. 'Toiletries, a fresh set of
clothing?'

'We can buy that.'

Her face tightened. 'It's not in my budget.'

'It is in mine. Millionaire, remember?' he
teased lightly. 'Come on, we barely ate at that
restaurant. See this as a continued thank you.'

'No,' she said softly. 'I know what this is.
You're being—' she hesitated '—kind. Hospita-
ble.'

'Yes,' he replied, relieved.

'I'll pay you back.'

'Piper—'

'I need to,' she interrupted firmly, but gently.
'It's important to me to be able to pay my way.'

'Of course,' he said. 'Fine, you can pay me
back.'

She nodded. 'Great. Now, what should we take
care of first?'

They sorted out a plan, first going to the super-market near the bus station to buy the essentials. Caleb packed in anything he thought she might want, claiming it was for himself. He didn't want her to pay him back, but he understood the prin-ciple of her wanting to. Respected it, too.

Perhaps it was wrong of him to want to buy things that he thought she might want, but he was okay with being wrong then. He wanted to make her happy, especially since he'd forced her into this. Well, Emma had, but he hadn't stopped it. In which case, this really was a thank you.

As they walked back up to the city, he stopped at one of the shops and bought a backpack. While he was at it, he bought a fresh set of clothes and swimming trunks. She chose a swimsuit for her-self when he told her he expected her to join him in the pool back at the house. He wanted her to get the full Greek experience, which meant straight exhaustion after a day of exploring.

They didn't buy anything after that, but Piper stopped at almost every shop, gushing over trin-kets and ornaments, sometimes over clothes. She spoke with the shopkeepers about the history of the island, about what they sold in their shop, and listened, even when their English was broken.

When they finally made it through the line of shops and were on their way to where Caleb wanted to watch the sunset, some stray dogs trotted towards them. He had to stop Piper when she immediately lowered to pet the dogs.

'They're street dogs.'

'Okay.' She looked at him with innocent eyes. 'What's wrong with me wanting to pet street dogs?'

'They live on the street.'

She blinked at him.

'No one takes care of them, Piper.'

'And that means they don't deserve love?' she asked. 'That's terrible. Shame on you.'

'That's not what I meant,' he said. 'They're dirty, unvaccinated and carry all kinds of diseases.' He softened his voice. 'It's not a good idea, Piper.'

Her face fell. It was adorable, damn it. Damn her.

'I hope you'll never find out what it's like to be alone and dirty and without love.'

'Me, too,' he said dryly.

She sighed. 'What if I just touch them with my—?'

'Piper.'

She glared at him, gave the dogs a longing look before sighing. 'Take me away from here, then.'

He smiled, leading her to another restaurant Adrian had taken him to when he'd first visited Greece.

'This is terrible,' she said when they sat down. 'Someone should take care of those dogs.'

'The government does, to an extent. There's food and water all around.'

'But what about shelters? Vaccines? Cleaning them?'

'You're an animal lover, I take it.'

She gave him a look. 'Yes. But I also have compassion. Why are you smiling? This is not amusing.'

'No, it's not,' he said after a moment, the smile fading.

It wasn't amusing at all that somehow, during this conversation, he'd decided he would look into setting up shelters for stray dogs in Greece.

CHAPTER TEN

WHO KNEW WATCHING a sunset with an incredibly attractive man could be so romantic?

Okay, she did.

In theory, it had seemed fine. Two acquaintances watching the sun set. But they weren't acquaintances. They were something more. Something that had become blurred as they'd spent time together. Like when Caleb had threaded his fingers through hers as the sun had set. Contentment had washed over her and she hadn't pulled away. Hadn't wanted to. Then there was the delicious dinner, the laughing, the sharing… Maybe that had added to the romance of it, too.

She could almost forget she was enjoying him when she shouldn't be.

She continued to forget it when they arrived at his place. It was, he told her, old Santorini architecture. The building was at the end of a road—no, she thought. It wasn't at the end of a road. The narrow track they'd driven along had essentially been an uncovered tunnel. There were, in fact, holes that looked like tunnels burrowed into the peak of the island, which apparently was a volcano.

'Are you telling me,' she said as he slowly drove down the ridiculous track to where he lived, 'that I am currently on an active volcano?'

'I am telling you that,' he said with a smirk. 'The island is what remained after a volcano erupted in the first place.'

'I'm still trying to wrap my head around the fact that it's an active volcano. Who the hell thought it was a good idea to turn it into a tourist destination?'

'I imagine the people who live here. Perhaps they saw the sunsets and figured people from around the world would want to see it.'

'It's a pretty great sunset,' she conceded. 'Although I'd rather be alive to see other sunsets than risk my life for one particular sunset. But that's just me, I guess.'

He chuckled, and again warmth ballooned inside her. She was getting too used to this. To hearing him laugh and seeing him smile. This after only a day. She could only imagine what would happen to her mind if she spent more time with him.

And she didn't only want to imagine it; she wanted to experience it.

The house offered a welcome distraction when he pulled up in front of it. It was a double storey, although the first storey wasn't level with the ground. They had to take steps down to get inside, though the second storey was above ground, making the design unique.

She walked into cool darkness. Caleb put on the lights, revealing concrete floors, modern appliances and décor, though the windows—round and high—looked old. A comfortable set of couches filled the living room, along with a TV and dining table. There were two bedrooms, one off the living room that had a king-sized bed and sliding doors that led out to the pool; another was upstairs, which was, when she followed Caleb up, essentially an entire apartment.

'You can stay here,' he told her, before explaining that the housekeeper had been round and Piper would have everything she needed. 'Shout if there is anything else though, and I'll try to organise it for you.'

'Thanks.'

'I'll see you at the pool in an hour?'

She smiled. 'Sure.'

He smiled back. It turned into a long moment of them simply smiling at one another, before Caleb awkwardly took a step back and missed falling down the stairs because of quick reflexes.

'I'll see you later,' he said, face flushing. He didn't wait for her to reply this time, only hurried down the stairs.

She was still smiling after her shower. To be

fair, that had just as much to do with his silliness as it did the fact that she could wash off the day and finally unwind. She had about forty minutes before she was supposed to meet Caleb, and she made the mistake of slipping into her sleepwear. She wanted to wait before putting on her swimming costume so she could be comfortable, but it meant that she was *comfortable*. The cool cotton bedding felt incredible. So did closing her eyes...

She woke up with a start, the inky darkness informing her she'd slept for much too long. Not that she'd intended to sleep at all. A quick glance at her phone told her it was midnight and she straightened, wondering how the hell she'd slept for four hours.

The house was quiet, which gave her plenty of opportunity to hear the voice in her head pointing out how poorly she'd slept for the last few weeks. She'd wondered if she should come to the wedding, had gone back and forth about it. But, as she'd told Caleb, she had no excuses. None, yet she'd kept trying to think of one. Deep into the night. For as long as two weeks before she'd flown. Longer, even. Every time she thought she didn't want to go, she saw Emma's disappointed expression, Liam's resigned one. Now she was here, looking for her brother, and she still wasn't sleeping well.

That was how she'd slept for four hours.

She padded into the kitchen, stopping when she saw a note on the table with her name on it. She picked it up.

Piper,
I want to say I'm mad about you falling asleep, but I get it. If you wake up before morning you'll probably be hungry. I left something for you in the fridge.
Caleb

Curious, she went over to the fridge. She took out the brown packaging, unwrapped the foil and gave a much too loud laugh when she saw what was inside.

A chicken sandwich.

When she was done laughing, she stared at the sandwich in her hand. Her chest felt funny. Warm. It took her a moment to realise it was because he'd done this for her. This…considerate, kind thing. Such actions always meant more to her because of the way she'd grown up. She knew that consideration and kindness shouldn't be taken for granted. She'd learnt that with Brad, too.

But Caleb… Caleb was both of those things. And he didn't have any qualms about displaying them with her. Towards her. Plus, she thought with a smile, he had a sense of humour. She rubbed her chest absently as she got a drink from the fridge. By the time she went outside to eat, she was almost used to the comfort of the warmth there. Which dissipated as soon as she noticed a figure sprawled in a lounger.

She made a tiny noise, before seeing it was Caleb. She managed to clamp down on any other sound when she realised he was sleeping. A voice in the back of her head told her she should walk away. Nothing good could come of watching him sleep. She'd notice he had fewer lines on his face, his body relaxed in a way she hadn't seen before. She'd see the smooth expanse of his chest, the muscular ridges since he lay there without his shirt on. His hair was untidy, a towel draped over his lap, and she assumed he'd gone for a swim without her.

So it hadn't only been a line to see her in her underwear.

Slowly, quietly, despite her warnings to herself, she lowered to another lounger and began eating her sandwich as quietly as possible. She was about to start her second half when he opened his eyes, started at seeing her, then straightened, rubbing a hand over the back of his neck.

'What time is it?'

'After twelve.'

'Midnight?' he said, shock wiping the sleepiness from his face. A pity. 'I've been sleeping here for two hours?'

'You went for a swim at ten?' She reached for her drink, gulping down some of it though she kept her eyes on him. 'You realise that's not normal?'

'I was hot.'

'Didn't you tell me there's air-conditioning?'

'Yeah, but it makes a loud buzzing noise. If you're not used to it, it might wake you up.'

The warmth returned to her chest, fiercer than before.

'Are you saying,' she said carefully, wanting to get it right, 'that you didn't put on the air-conditioning because you were afraid of waking me up?'

'Yeah,' he said, shifting in his lounger and running a hand over his hair now. 'You wouldn't have fallen asleep if you weren't tired,' he added. 'I figured you needed as much of it as you could get.'

She nodded, still processing.

'And you left me a chicken sandwich in case I woke up.'

'I thought you might be hungry.'

'Hmm.'

She studied him—his bare chest, his mussed hair. It made her realise the warmth she was feeling was attraction just as much as everything else. And the everything else was significant on its own.

It was responsible for that pull. The one she'd first felt when they'd been climbing the steps to Oia. Only it was stronger now. It tempted her to get up, slide her hands into his hair and rest her lips on his.

She cleared her throat. 'That was nice of you.'

'I can be nice,' he said good-naturedly. 'Are you going to eat the rest of that?'

She looked down, only then realising she hadn't finished her sandwich. She shook her head, lifted her plate in a *you can have it* gesture. He got up, lowered next to her on her lounger. It became a little harder to breathe.

'It's pretty good,' he said after his first bite. He took a second before she could answer.

'Yeah,' she said, her voice strangled.

'Why does your expression make me think you're lying?'

'It's not the sandwich.'

He took the last bite with a frown. Finished chewing before he asked, 'Then what is it?'

'Nothing.'

Involuntarily, her eyes lowered to his lips, before she shifted her gaze. What was happening to her? A day in the presence of this man and she was losing all the progress she'd made after Brad.

Except this, him? It felt like progress. He might have been controlling, but it didn't have the same malice Brad had. Brad wouldn't have cared if she was sleeping; he'd still have made noise. He wouldn't have considered she might be hungry if she woke up. He certainly wouldn't have been looking for her brother when Liam was the one in the wrong…

Or was she making excuses? Was she ignoring the alarm bells with Caleb because of the attraction they shared? Not only the attraction: the connection. That pull.

'I have… I need to…'

She didn't finish her sentence, only moved forward and tried to stand. But Caleb stood at the same time, and her urgency to get away from him—to escape the thoughts and the *feelings*—propelled her against his chest. Against his bare chest.

'Piper.'

His voice was soft. Gruff. It sent shivers down her spine.

'What?' she whispered, forcing herself not to look at his lips.

'What's wrong?'

'Nothing.'

'Piper.' He said her name on a sigh this time. 'You don't have to lie to me.'

'No, I do,' she said urgently. 'If I lie to you, maybe I can lie to myself.'

'About what?'

He brushed a strand of hair from her face. She closed her eyes, resisted—barely—leaning into his hand.

'This,' she said, looking at him. 'I want to lie about whatever this is.'

Caleb's expression didn't change, but it was only then that she realised what his expression was. A tenderness that soothed her heart. Her fears. A desire that sent another shiver down her spine.

'Don't lie,' he said softly. 'This doesn't have to be anything you don't want it to be.'

'That's the problem.' She slid her arms around his waist, rested her head against his chest. 'I want it to be.'

She didn't have to clarify the 'it'. The word, the hope, sat heavy between them. After a moment, Caleb's arms folded around her waist, and it happened again. That wave of contentment. That feeling of safety. She wasn't sure how it happened, but she didn't want it to end. So when she pulled back, she didn't lift her eyes to his. She let them linger on his lips. They were full, sensual. And when they lowered to hers, she gave a murmur of assent.

The touching of their lips was soft, though there was no tentativeness about it. She felt a vibration go through her, realised a second later it was Caleb's groan. She understood his reaction. That soft touching of their lips had sparked a wild desire inside her, too.

It shifted things. Made the kiss become more urgent than exploratory. It made everything more…*more*.

His tongue slid into her mouth; she felt an

answering flicker of heat low in her belly. She cupped his neck with her hand, drawing him closer, giving herself more access. The world rumbled beneath them. She wondered if the volcano island had erupted after all. Strangely, now, she wasn't as concerned about dying.

His hands were on her skin, creating paths, trails she'd retrace when this was over and she was clinging to the memory. For now, she had the fire of it. An almost lazy one that burnt while the rest of her simmered. A juxtaposition that made no sense: the temperature was rising inside her with each sweep of his tongue, his hands responsible for the outside of her body recreating the supernova.

It was intoxicating, this man's talent. He knew how to kiss, how to caress. She was surprised she hadn't fallen prey to his charms earlier since he was clearly an expert at seduction. Now that he was aiming it at her, she was content in a way she'd never been before. Riled up in that way, too.

She didn't think about the firsts of it. Instead, she tentatively put her hands on his torso. The muscles beneath her fingers clenched. Trembled. It had desire quaking through her, the power of it impossible to ignore.

She was doing this. She was making this attractive, confident man tremble.

She pressed closer to him, lifting her hands

to cup his face. It shifted the tone again, this time from seductive to emotional. From eager to grateful.

The movement of their tongues slowed. His hands stilled. And though she was aching she was able to catch her breath. Only for him to make her lose it again when he pulled back and rested his forehead on hers.

'This is…' he said, his voice husky. She felt pride tingle inside her.

'I know.'

'Are you okay with it?'

'Don't I seem okay?'

His eyes searched her face. 'I need you to say it.'

Softening, she said, 'I'm more than okay. This is more than I could have imagined.'

He smiled at her. 'Good. Because I wasn't done.'

She laughed. 'Me neither. I—'

She shut up when he picked her up.

His gaze flickered down to her. 'Objections?'

'None,' she said, voice shaky. Then she realised how close she was to him and began to trace the lines of his face. 'You don't look annoyed with me.'

'You want me to be annoyed with you?' he asked, amusement dancing in his expression. 'I'm sure that'll come. Keep talking. That's one way to get me there, for sure.'

'Hmm.' She narrowed her eyes. 'Maybe *I* should be annoyed with you. You do seem to have a gift for annoying me.'

He smiled, lowering his head to nip at her lips. 'Later. There are more important things now.'

He carried her through the sliding doors to his bedroom. Gently lowered her to his bed. Her heart pounded at the prospect of what might happen until he lay on the bed beside her and only looked at her.

'This is more important?'

He put a warm hand on her waist. 'It is.'

Warmth spread through her body, but not in the achy way kissing him had caused. No, this was different. Soothing. Gentle. She knew it was just as dangerous.

'I won't lie,' she said, shifting closer to him. 'I thought there would be more action.'

'There's time for action.'

'Really? When?'

'Now,' he replied. 'Ten minutes from now. In an hour. Tomorrow.'

'I'm not sure tomorrow's a possibility.'

'Why not?'

'I might have come to my senses by then.'

'Or maybe this *is* you coming to your senses.'

She stared at him, laughed quietly. 'You're good.'

He smiled. 'I know.'

'Cocky though.'

'You say that like it's a bad thing.'

'It might be,' she said, remembering.

Popping the bubble.

She cursed silently and turned onto her back, facing the ceiling. There was a fan there. She had no idea why, when there was air-conditioning. Perhaps it was for moments like this, when the doors were open. Or when a man didn't want to put on the air-conditioning because he was afraid to wake his grumpy companion.

Damn it. The thought of it sent another wave of pleasure through her. And it was probably why she was lying on her brother's future brother-in-law's bed, thinking about the men in her past.

'I'm sorry,' Caleb said suddenly, sitting up. 'I shouldn't have brought you inside here. You're uncomfortable.' He let out a breath. 'I'm messing things up.'

'No, you're not,' she said, pushing up on her hands. 'I am. I mean, I did. I hope not to any more.'

'You want to stay?'

'I want to stay,' she said simply.

After a long moment of silence where he studied her, he nodded and lowered back to the bed. She noticed that his body was tense now, that he'd moved away from her slightly. She sighed, lowering to her back again, resting her hands on her belly.

'My father,' she started, thinking the only way

to make things easier was to explain, 'was…a challenge to live with.'

She felt him turn, face her again. But he didn't speak, and she had to commend him for giving her the space to figure it out.

'You know that already. And that my mother died when Liam and I were young. I… I don't think my father knew what to do with us. Or maybe it was simply that he didn't want us.' Her stomach twisted. She pushed on. 'He was very controlling. He'd punish us if we stepped outside of what he wanted us to do. It was like living on the top of a very narrow mountain. One wrong step and we'd fall long and hard to the ground.'

'He hurt you?' Caleb's voice was dangerously devoid of emotion.

She turned her head. 'You mean physically?' she asked. He nodded. 'No, he never hit us.' She looked up again. Wished the fan was on so she'd have something to look at. Something to distract her from the memories. 'We never had physical bruises.'

'Only emotional ones.'

She'd implied it, but it pleased her that he'd seen it. 'Yes.'

'How did you survive it?'

'I didn't take any steps,' she replied. 'I stayed on one spot on the mountain.' She paused. 'I used to walk around, but it wasn't worth the fall.'

'Was staying worth it?'

She angled her head. 'I don't… I don't know. I suppose I survived it, which is important. But I carry it with me, and it's so heavy sometimes.' She fell silent. 'I eventually moved. Fell.' Another pause. 'He didn't want me to go to university. He wanted me to stay home and take care of him.' She shook her head. 'I couldn't. When Liam left and didn't come back, I realised I was the only person who could get myself out of that situation. So I got a job, fought to leave, tried to find independence.'

'Did you?'

She thought about Brad. 'Not quite.'

'What happened?'

'I made a mistake.' She looked at him. 'I spent the entirety of my degree alone. Then my father died, and I didn't want to be alone any more. It was like…like his death gave me permission to… I don't know, date?' She rolled her eyes at the stupidity of it. 'But I dated the wrong man. Turns out, having a crappy male role model your entire life gives you a pretty skewed view of yourself and the people you should date.'

His brow knitted, and she could almost see him applying it to his situation.

'That didn't happen with your sisters,' she told him.

'No, but sometimes I wonder if I gave them other issues.'

'Like what?'

'I don't know.' He went quiet. 'I've spoilt them. And now they can't do things by themselves.'

'It's not too late.'

He gave her a dark look. 'I'm here looking for my sister's fiancé.'

'So am I,' she pointed out. 'Not my sister's fi— Oh, you know what I mean.'

He laughed softly. 'I do.'

'Why did you spoil them?'

'My father died.'

'And you thought it would help with their grief?'

'Yeah.'

'Did it?'

She gave him time to think about it when she saw his expression. The pain there. The confusion. Guilt, too, if she wasn't mistaken. All of it gave her a new understanding of Caleb. Of what he was doing for his siblings.

She'd been judging him according to her frame of reference, according to her past, but perhaps it was time to use his frame of reference. He'd had to parent his siblings. His father had died more than a decade ago; he probably hadn't been that old when that responsibility had come his way.

What if his control was a coping mechanism? What if he'd had to control things, to be a parent when he'd barely been an adult?

'I don't know,' he finally answered.

'And you feel guilty about it.'

He looked at her, his expression unguarded. 'I feel guilty. But not because of that.'

CHAPTER ELEVEN

SHE SAW RIGHT through him. He wanted to ask her how, but he didn't know if he'd like the answer. They were in a bubble. It had started inflating the moment they'd had dinner at sunset. Perhaps even before then. But everything had felt easy and significant, in a way he couldn't describe.

It wouldn't end well.

He should have known it when he'd walked into her bedroom after waiting ten minutes at the pool. He'd seen her curled into a ball in the middle of the sheets. She wore a soft blue sleep shirt and, with her gorgeous brown skin, made a picture on the white bedding. But it was her face that got him. The barriers had been lowered—the scowl she always wore gone, the carefulness in her eyes not visible. It had kicked him in the gut. Made him want to take care of her.

He'd only ever had that feeling with his siblings. Feeling it for a stranger…was weird. Especially now, when it was more intense after he'd heard what her father—her *brother*—had done to her. No wonder he was feeling vulnerable.

Not that he was running away from it. In fact, he was embracing it. The bubble was that powerful.

'You don't have to feel guilty, you know,' she said. 'I don't think their grief is keeping them from doing anything in their lives. I have no doubt that's because of you.'

'That's not it,' he said slowly.

'What then?'

'Having my dad.'

There was a stunned pause. He used it to figure out how he'd just told her the thing he'd never been able to say out loud.

'What do you mean?'

He took a breath. 'I mean I feel guilty for having him for eighteen years of my life, and they didn't get nearly as many.'

'That wasn't your fault.'

'I know.' Another breath. This was harder than he'd anticipated. 'He was such a great dad, Piper. He was strict, but supportive. He was patient, and when he got things wrong, he'd say so.' He relaxed the fingers that had clenched the sheets. 'He wasn't perfect, but he tried. And Em, Jada and Tate should have someone who tries, too.'

'Is that why you're looking for Liam?' she asked. 'Why you're so involved with this wedding? Why you picked me up?'

'Yeah, I guess so.'

'Sounds…tough. Trying to be your father, I mean.'

'No. Just trying.'

'Okay.'

He didn't reply. Knew she knew her comment had already done what it was meant to. Facing it brought more guilt. But this was the bubble, wasn't it? Maybe he could finally say what he'd been feeling…

'It's exhausting,' he admitted, relief crashing into him. 'I don't think I can be him. But I still think I should try, because they deserve that. But look what they turned into. Adults who rely on their brother for everything. I know I did that, and I wish I hadn't. I wish…'

Shame kept him from continuing. But a warm hand closed over his, squeezing gently. He turned to see a non-judgemental expression on Piper's face. One that made him feel safe, despite his shame.

'I wish they didn't need me so much,' he whispered.

She cupped his cheek. 'You've taken on so much responsibility, haven't you?'

'My mother left when the kids were young. My dad died. What was I supposed to do?'

'Be a little selfish?'

'That's not an option.' He shook his head. 'My

dad stepped up when my mother died. I had to do the same when he died.'

'And you did.' Her thumb brushed his cheek. 'Maybe it's time you let them step up, too.'

'This is scary,' he said, his voice ragged. From the realisations, the hope—he wasn't sure.

'Yeah.' There was a pause. 'I've never told anyone about what happened with my father. Or my brother.'

'He should have been there for you,' Caleb said, because he needed to.

She smiled. 'I'm here for him now. Hopefully that will change things.'

'You're here for a reconciliation?'

'Heavens, no.' She shook her head for good measure. 'I didn't want to come, remember? A reconciliation didn't even occur to me before this point.'

'Why did it now?'

'You,' she said simply. 'Your love for your siblings is… I guess it's something I'd like in my life, too.' She shrugged. 'You have to be willing to give before you can get, and all that.'

He turned to face her, shifting closer.

'I don't know how you feel about being here any more,' he said softly, 'but I'm very happy you are.'

'Right now,' she whispered back, shifting closer to him, too, 'so am I.'

Their lips touching this time was more of a sigh

than a shout. It was tender, affectionate. Full of what they couldn't say to one another. Or perhaps full of what they had said to one another.

He put his hand back on the waist he'd had a brief feel of earlier. Now that she was lying, he could memorise the dip of it. That valley between her breasts and her hips. It was the perfect place to stop, to appreciate; he did neither. Instead, he ran his hand over the curve of her. The entirety of her side, from her shoulder down to her hand. Back up, over the side of her chest, her waist, her hips.

She shook beneath his caresses, and damn if he didn't think making her shake was the most important thing he'd ever done in his life. Her hands were on his chest, his bare skin absorbing the heat of it, sending it in pulses of pleasure into his body. He thanked the heavens that he'd fallen asleep after his swim. That he hadn't been able to cover himself.

If he hadn't he wasn't sure he'd have the pleasure of her skin on his. He didn't want to push her, wouldn't have wanted to remove his shirt because of it. It would have been a travesty not to know. Fortunately, he did know.

He cherished the tentative strokes of her hands against his skin. Cherished it as humans might have cherished fire when it had first been discovered. The feel of it was hot and dangerous, but he couldn't move away. He didn't want to move away. So he would stay even though he knew eventually he would burn. It would be worth it.

A groan slipped from his lips when her hands went around his waist and she pulled him closer. Their bodies were flush against one another. There was no hiding how he felt about what they were doing. How he felt about her, since this wasn't just another night with another woman— it was *this* night.

With her.

'I don't think I'm ready to sleep with you yet,' she said, pulling away from him. Her chest was moving quickly against his. She wasn't wearing a bra, which meant he could feel... He could *feel*.

Suddenly he was clinging to that *yet* more than any grown man should.

'Okay,' he said, his voice sounding foreign to him. 'We don't have to.'

'But maybe we could do some other stuff.'

'Stuff,' he repeated, his brain malfunctioning.

She laughed, a hoarse, sexy sound that had his senses scrambling while his body said *yes*.

The morning after was always awkward. Or so the movies she watched told her. They were not accurate in this case.

Sure, she and Caleb hadn't had sex. But they'd done...*stuff*, which was as intimate. At least for her, since this wasn't the kind of thing she did. Outside of Brad, she'd had no romantic relationships. No romantic liaisons either. It had been her choice, one made from fear, yes, but also power.

For the first time in her life she could choose what she wanted and who she wanted to be around. It was fantastic. Her evening with Caleb seemed to prove it.

So did the morning.

She woke up to find him still there, sprawled under the sheet they'd pulled over themselves in the early morning. The clock told her they'd had about five hours of sleep. It was nowhere near enough, but she felt rested. More relaxed than she'd ever been. There was a brief moment when she thought about Liam and their meeting, but that was still hours away. She shoved it to the back of her mind. She'd deal with it when she had to. For now, she had a gorgeous man to stare at.

She'd managed all of two minutes before he woke up, smiled at her and pulled her into his arms.

'Breakfast,' he said in a gravelly voice that sounded way too sexy for first thing in the morning.

'Yes,' she told him with a quiet chuckle. 'I'll make something.'

'No,' he said when she moved to leave his arms.

She relaxed against his chest. 'We have to get up some time. Considering you're hungry and all.'

'I know.' He pressed a kiss into her hair. She winced. 'What?' he asked.

'It needs to be washed.'

'Would you like to do that?'

'Yes, very much so.'

'Okay, we'll shower. But only because I want to kiss your hair some more and I don't want you wincing every time I do. Plus, there's that food thing.'

'Did you say *we'll* shower?' she asked carefully.

He smiled. 'In our two different showers, yes. Unless…'

'It's going to be harder than that to get me to do your bidding,' she said, moving out of the arms he'd slackened. She widened her eyes as she climbed out of the bed. 'And to think I wasn't even trying to make a dirty joke with that. It just…worked.'

She missed the pillow he threw at her by leaping out of the way at the last second, and went to her room laughing.

'We'll go out for breakfast,' he called out. 'Wear something nice.'

Since she only had one option of clothing, she didn't respond. Her body sang as the hot water heated it, her head thanking her when she dipped it under the steam and rinsed out the coconut oil. She silently thanked Caleb for insisting she bought the things she needed for her hair when they were out shopping. She'd tried to save money, and a sulphate-free shampoo and conditioner seemed like an unnecessary expense when she had full bottles back at the villa.

'I'll use it when you're done,' Caleb had said, plucking the bottle from the shelf.

She'd eyed his close-cut hairstyle. 'You're going to use it on—what? Your scalp?'

'Sulphate dries my scalp out, so yeah, I guess so.'

Thoroughly chastised, she hadn't argued.

She didn't like wearing her hair loose when it was curly. It was long and thick, which meant her curls went everywhere when it wasn't blow-dried straight. She did her best to tame it with the conditioner, then, when that took too long, she put a band over her wrist and hurried down to Caleb.

She missed him already, which made no sense, but she didn't question it. She wasn't questioning anything until she met her brother and everything changed. Tension pulled at her stomach but she stomped down on it. She smiled when she went onto the patio and found Caleb waiting for her.

'Hey,' she said. 'I know you said *nice,* which I think this is since we both decided on— What?' she asked, when his eyes went wide as he looked at her. 'What's wrong?'

'Your hair.'

'Oh.' Self-consciously, she lifted a hand to it. 'I was about to tie it up,' she said, gathering the curls.

'No,' he said, moving forward. 'Don't.'

She stopped, lowering her hands awkwardly.

'This is what your hair looks like wet?'

'When it's not blow-dried, yeah.'

'It's...'

She held her breath.

'Beautiful. Breathtaking, actually. That's what I was trying to say. I was hoping for something more eloquent.'

'That was plenty eloquent,' she said in a small voice as pleasure filled her. It cleared her brain, told her that that expression she'd first seen on Caleb's face had been awe, not disgust.

'Did you think I'd say something else?' he asked, drawing her in with an arm around her waist. With his free hand, he played with the curls. There was a joy on his face that healed a wound she hadn't known was inside her.

'No,' she lied.

Caleb's expression changed. It was so slight that she couldn't be sure, especially when he quickly smiled. When he pressed a soft kiss to her lips. 'It's extraordinary. You're extraordinary.'

'So,' she said, stepping back as the warmth did its thing in her chest. 'What's for breakfast?'

'You'll see,' he said with a grin.

They drove the complicated road to the beach in silence. It was easy, companionable, and allowed her to enjoy the sight of the sand stretched in front of the dark blue sea. The sea crashed into the mountain on its left, and a row of restaurants and beach recliners sat on its right.

'This is beautiful,' she said when they sat down. Caleb had headed straight to this restaurant and she'd followed, because she assumed he'd brought her there for a reason.

'Isn't it?'

He smiled at her and picked up the menu, reading his recommendations to her. They ordered, and when the waiter left Caleb took her hand.

'You lied to me earlier,' he said softly.

'What?' she asked, warmth quickly freezing in her chest.

'When I asked you about your hair. You were lying about what you thought my reaction would be.'

'Oh.' She took a breath. 'Well, yes, but we were having such a nice time. I didn't want to —'

'You don't have to lie about your past,' he interrupted.

'Oh.' It was strange being with someone who said things she needed to hear. Or who made her feel comfortable enough that she didn't feel ashamed when he chided her. 'I'm sorry I lied. I didn't want to spoil the moment.'

'Tell me now.'

She hesitated. Sighed. 'My father, my ex-boyfriend… They disapproved of me wearing my hair curly.'

'Your ex-boyfriend… You dated someone like your father?'

Though she'd been expecting it, hearing the words hurt her. They were an accusation, even though he hadn't meant them to be. This was why she didn't want to think about her past. She knew she would be reminded of her mistakes. Her stupidity.

'Yes,' she said, as unaffectedly as she could manage. 'I told you I had some relationship trouble.'

'You didn't say it was this kind of trouble.'

She studied him. 'You're wondering why I would date someone like my father.'

The waiter brought their drinks. When he left, Piper began to trace patterns into the menu.

'You don't have to answer if you don't want to.'

Caleb's eyes were warm. Supportive.

So she gave him an answer.

'I didn't see it. He wasn't exactly like my father. Especially not at first.'

'He lied to you?'

'He manipulated me,' she replied, though they were two sides of the same coin. 'It was easy to do. He was the first man to pay attention to me when I had my freedom. When I could actually do something about it, I mean,' she added. 'We went out a few months before the suggestions started. And they *were* suggestions at first.' She took a breath. 'Well, he gave me choices, which I suppose isn't the same thing.'

She flipped the menu, smoothing out the lamination. Not that it was necessary.

'But those choices felt like suggestions. That… that felt like freedom. To someone who didn't have choices growing up, choosing felt like freedom. Even when the options were predetermined.' She felt faintly sick about it, even now. 'It was years before I realised that. And who he was.' She shook out her shoulders. 'It's done now, and I'm over it.'

He smiled. It was an indulgent smile, and it told her he didn't believe her. She couldn't even blame him. She *wasn't* over it. Not when the fear of repeating those mistakes still haunted every decision she made.

'You know,' she said after a moment, 'I probably shouldn't have told you this. Not when you're having an existential crisis of your own.'

'I'm not—' He broke off. Scowled at her. 'Is it too late to stay in bed?'

'Afraid so.'

CHAPTER TWELVE

HE DIDN'T SHOW.

Caleb tried not to be annoyed with Liam, considering what Piper had told him about their childhood. He could see that feeling trapped might be a problem for Liam. Could see that his fiancée telling him they had a house and would soon have a baby could make him feel trapped.

He tried, but he didn't succeed.

'I wonder if he's made a will. If he has, I hope he left something to you. Most of it should go to Emma,' he said, 'but you should get some, too. After I kill him, I mean.'

'Some of what?' Piper asked dully. 'The profits of his failed businesses? Or his debts? With my luck, that would be the only thing he's left me.' She blew out a breath. 'This is getting tedious now.'

'You're telling me.'

'It should mean something that he's pitching up, though?' she asked, holding the note Liam had left. This one just said, *Sorry, I'll be in touch soon.* 'Yes, I know I'm clutching at straws,' she said in response to the look he shot her. 'I'm trying to stay positive. It's getting harder. The wedding's two days away.'

'And there are festivities.'

'Festivities?' she repeated.

'Yes.' He grimaced. 'Emma wanted a countdown party for every day until the wedding day. Three, two, one,' he clarified.

'Tonight's two?'

'Today's two,' he corrected. 'In a few hours, we're all supposed to meet at the lighthouse in Mykonos. A photoshoot followed by drinks on the dock until sunset. Dinner, then partying until day one.'

'What happened yesterday? Day three?' She didn't wait for him to answer. 'And what'll happen tomorrow?'

'Much of the same,' he said with a sigh. 'I should probably call her and tell her he's not here.'

'No,' she said. 'Let's wait until he gets in touch before we tell her anything.'

'She'll worry.'

'I know, but she's worried now anyway. At least if we wait, she'll have hope. And we might have something to tell her.'

'The news isn't becoming more positive.'

'It might.'

She said it so hopefully he gave in.

'Fine, but I have to call Jada to update her. She

and Tate are in charge of the guests on the island—' He broke off with a wince. 'This is ugly.'

She patted his arm as he made the call. More comfort, although he wished he didn't need it. He didn't want to be calling any of his siblings with bad news. He'd done it when they'd lost their father, and that had been more than enough for his entire lifetime.

Or so he wanted to believe.

'Please tell me you have good news,' Jada said when she answered.

'No.'

She heaved a sigh. 'Figures. Otherwise you'd be calling Em, not me.'

'How is she?'

'How do you think?' Jada asked dryly. 'She's two months pregnant and her fiancé is MIA. He might not make it to the wedding.'

He could almost hear Jada rolling her eyes.

'I'm staying in Santorini for the day. We might have a lead, so we're waiting to see how it pans out. Is everything going okay with the countdown party?'

'You mean, besides the bride and groom being on an imaginary pre-wedding trip on their own? And also the bride's brother and the groom's sister being conspicuously missing? Yeah, it is.' There was a pause. 'You and Piper are getting along, then?'

Heat immediately curled around his neck. He angled his body away from Piper's.

'Yes.'

'Yes? That's it?'

'Yes.'

'Oh, I get it. She's nearby.'

'Yes.'

'So you're getting along, huh?'

'I already said yes to that.'

'How well?'

'If you've got everything sorted for tonight, I'll let you go annoy someone else.'

'*That* well? Wow, Caleb, you move really fast.'

'Goodbye, Jada.'

He put down the phone, though he could hear her still speaking. Piper gave him an amused look.

'So, she's teasing you about me?'

'How did you know?'

'You're blushing,' she said. 'You angled away from me when, I'm guessing, she started asking about me.'

He felt his colour deepen. Scowled because of it.

She patted his arm, though now it was condescending, not comforting.

'I'm a teacher, Caleb. I deal with this kind of thing all the time.'

'You don't have to be so self-satisfied about it.'

She laughed. It sounded delightful. He wouldn't show her that.

'I do enjoy using my skills outside the classroom. Makes me feel like my education wasn't wasted.' Her eyes glistened with amusement and, damn it, he couldn't resist smiling at her. Then her eyes shifted to behind him and she grinned. 'Ice cream! Let's go get some.'

He knew she was trying to distract him. Since he was currently eating butterscotch ice cream, he figured she'd succeeded. More so since she'd chosen her ice cream in a cone, and the movement of her tongue was mesmerising. He averted his eyes so he wouldn't embarrass himself.

'So what now?' he asked when his gaze slipped back to her.

'I don't know,' she said with a sigh. 'We have to stay in phone range. We probably also have to stay on the island since Liam might still be here.'

'Doesn't give us too many options.'

'True.'

They both went silent.

'What if we go back to the beach and wait it out there?' she asked. 'I mean, there could be worse things.'

His brow knitted. 'Did you see the stones on that beach? It's not swimmer-friendly.'

'You're comparing it to Cape Town beaches,' she scolded him. 'Those rocks are part of the experience here.'

'I'm not cutting my foot on a rock for the experience.'

'This from the person who wanted a donkey to take us up more than a hundred steps.'

'That was safe. Have you ever heard of death by donkey in Greece?' he asked at her lifted eyebrows.

'No, but I haven't looked. I'm sure I'll find it.'

'I'm still not swimming with rocks.'

'How did you create such a successful business when you're so risk averse?'

'I take risks,' he defended himself. 'They're a lot easier to take when it's business.'

Or when your livelihood and sanity depend on it.

He didn't say it. She didn't need to know how the business had been a blessing and curse after his father's death. It had given him something else to focus on, but it had reminded him of his father. And of his new responsibilities, since if he messed up at work his siblings wouldn't live the life he'd been lucky enough to live when his father had still been alive.

He released a breath. He needed to move on from this. And though he had no doubt it would be hard, he thought letting his siblings stand on their own might be the place to start. Even the thought of it gave him anxiety.

He was relieved that Piper didn't notice his turmoil. As they drove back to the beach, she chattered about this and that, making astute if irrelevant observations about the island.

'Can you imagine learning to drive here?' she asked when a car pulled in front of them without warning. 'No rules, no laws. Each person for themselves.'

'This isn't the Wild West, Piper,' he said with a laugh. 'There are rules.'

'Really?' Her voice dripped with sarcasm. 'Please do tell me what they are as I cannot for the life of me see order in this. There aren't even robots here.'

'I think they'd call it traffic lights.'

'Yes, but what does it matter, since they don't have them?'

He laughed again, and the tension he'd felt earlier faded. He should probably start putting distance between him and Piper. Stop enjoying her company so much. Stop letting her make him feel better. As soon as they got back to Mykonos, their bubble would pop. And they would fall—hard, he had no doubt. But maybe if he pulled away now... If he guarded himself against the inevitability of it...

Then Piper said something that made her laugh, and he knew he couldn't do it. How could he resist that bright and happy laugh? How could he resist someone who made *themselves* laugh in that way? He was too far gone to be guarded. She'd already crept under the barriers. Ones he'd only now realised he'd erected.

The discovery drew him into his thoughts.

Piper must have realised he'd stopped listening because she stopped talking, too. The silence that followed wasn't uncomfortable. It felt pregnant, as though one of them might break it at any moment. Neither of them did. By the time they got to the beach, Caleb worried he'd broken something by not talking. Until he looked over and saw Piper was sleeping.

She'd woken up before him that morning, and he hadn't got the opportunity to see her like this. Up close. It was probably why he hadn't minded that she'd been watching him sleep. When he'd woken up and seen her looking at him, he'd immediately understood. He would have done the same thing if he could.

Because he could now, he did. She took his breath away. Awake, more so, because he could add the light in her eyes when she was teasing him, the quirk of her eyebrow when she was challenging him. It lit a fire inside him—one fuelled by annoyance and attraction and desire. More dangerous than the fire was the fierce wave of protectiveness that extinguished it in moments he least expected it to.

When she'd come out of the house that morning with her long thick curls forming a curtain around her face, her shoulders, she'd taken his breath away. The fire had raged, this time entirely from attraction, desire. Of course, that was partly due to how they'd spent the night before. To how waking up with her in the morning had felt.

But then she'd lost all her confidence and spark when she'd asked him about it. Her reasons— her past—made him angry. He didn't know what to do with that anger. It crackled whenever he thought about the emotional abuse she'd endured. She hadn't said it was that, but what she'd told him was a clear example of it. He wished he could go back and protect her from it. Which had the anger blazing again when he realised she *had* someone who could have protected her. He simply chose not to.

These last two days had not been good for his opinion of his future brother-in-law. Though at this point Caleb was hesitant to call Liam even that.

'Piper,' he said, his voice hoarse. He cleared his throat. 'Piper,' he said again.

Her eyes opened, softened when they saw him. It did him in and he leaned forward, kissing her. She made a soft noise before lifting her hands and cupping his face. The meeting of their tongues felt meaningful, more than the night before. He wasn't sure how that was possible, but he embraced it. Channelled all the confusion about what he felt for her into the movement of their mouths.

When he pulled back she smiled at him. It was

a shy smile, a happy smile. His heart filled with pleasure.

'What was that for?' she asked.

'You're beautiful.'

Joy burst from her face, flooding her cheeks with colour. 'You're not too bad yourself.'

He smiled. 'Good to know.'

'Out of all your siblings, you're at least in the top two handsome men.'

He laughed. 'You certainly know how to put a man in his place, don't you?'

'Not any man,' she said serenely. 'Only you. Since I've met you, I've wanted to do nothing else.'

He rolled his eyes, but he didn't bother hiding his smile. He would enjoy her. Time was running out on how long he could.

She felt bad. Mostly because she knew what was happening back on the island of Mykonos. Tate and Jada were desperately trying to keep the guests from finding out her brother had run away from his pregnant fiancée. Emma was heartbroken. Not to mention that Liam was somewhere out there, trying to wrap his head around what his life would become.

She, on the other hand? She was enjoying an ice-cold cocktail with the most attractive man she'd ever seen. On the beach. Under an umbrella that kept her out of direct sunlight but didn't keep her from the heat of the sun.

She sighed in pleasure—and guilt—and turned her head to Caleb.

'This is wrong. We should be doing something more than this to find Liam.'

'Is your phone on?' he replied.

'Yeah.'

'Do you have signal?'

She checked. 'Yes.'

'Battery?'

'Yes.'

'What could we do besides that?'

His chest rose and fell with his breath. He'd taken off his shirt, and she got distracted by the muscles before answering his question.

'I don't know, but I feel like the answer should be more than this.'

He took her hand, brought it to his lips. He enjoyed doing that; she enjoyed having him do it. No—she loved that he did it. She loved the easy affection. It was a new experience for her. Brad hadn't believed in PDA, even small ones like this. She'd dated him for years and not once had they held hands in public. How had she not seen that as a red flag?

'I know this is strange, considering everything. Believe me, there's nothing more I want to do than to find Liam and get some answers. But our best bet is waiting for that phone call. I don't want to waste my time running around the island, only to discover he's not here.'

'So you'd rather waste your time on the beach with me?'

'There's no one I'd rather waste my time with,' he replied with a smile.

She shook her head. 'You need to work on how amusing you think you are.'

'You need to work on your sense of humour.'

He winked at her before putting his sunglasses back on and slipping down on the beach chair. She didn't laugh, didn't smile, though she did both on the inside. She complimented her self-control, right until the moment she stuck her tongue out at him.

'I saw that,' he said lazily.

'You were supposed to.'

He laughed, and she lowered onto her own beach chair, letting the heat soothe her body. They stayed like that for hours, sipping drinks, ordering food. When it got too hot, they walked down to the beach front shops and bought another pair of swimsuits. Piper didn't complain this time. She didn't want to spoil their afternoon.

She did protest at the costume Caleb selected for her though. A piece of string, essentially, that she gave her opinion on with a single look. He laughed, tried again with an equally revealing bikini. She ignored him and chose something she was more comfortable with. They changed and went for the swim. She didn't even mention Caleb's fear of hurting himself on the rocks…

Oh, who was she kidding? She mentioned it several times, particularly when she swam towards him, wrapping her legs around his waist.

'I should leave you here to fend for yourself,' he said when she teased him yet again. They were in deep waters, Caleb easily keeping them up with his strokes.

'By all means,' she said. 'I'm sure there'll be at least one gentleman who'd be interested in picking up where you left off.' She pretended to look around. 'Maybe that one over there? Sir,' she called loudly. 'Sir, would you be interested in—'

He cut her off with a kiss, and she giggled into his mouth, a free sound she'd never heard come from herself before.

'Keep going,' Caleb said, his eyes hot. 'I would love to keep you from talking some more.'

'Your suggestion has been noted,' she said lightly. 'Alternative suggestion. How about we just keep making out? No excuses.'

'I like the way you think.'

Their lips met again, and they kissed until Caleb forgot he was keeping them up and they both slipped under the water. Laughing, they left the ocean. It was sunset by then, the start of the evening punctuated by loud traditional Greek music.

Night fell as they were having dinner. Locals and tourists alike filled the road between the restaurants and the beach. There was laughter and breaking plates. Loud chattering, dancing, fun. It was the kind of scene shown in movies, and Piper felt incredibly happy to witness it in real life. More so to witness it with Caleb.

Then her phone rang.

'Liam,' she answered immediately, ignoring the tension that grabbed her entire body. 'Where are you?'

'Hello?' came a voice. 'Pie? I can't hear you.'

She gestured to the crowd for Caleb's sake, stood and left the restaurant. She manoeuvred through the people until she could find a quiet spot. It was some metres away, and she told Liam to stay on the line.

'Hey,' she said once she finally found a quiet place. 'Sorry about that. It's loud out here tonight.'

'You're at the countdown party?' he asked.

'Um,' she said, only just remembering that he didn't know where she was. 'No. I'm still in Santorini. I thought I'd wait in case you're still here. Are you?'

'Yeah.'

'Okay.' There was a pause. 'Can we meet up?'

'You're not alone, are you?'

She sighed. 'No. Emma wanted Caleb to come with me.'

There was a long stretch of silence. The only way she knew he was still on the phone was because she could hear his breathing.

'He's mad, huh?'

'Why are you worrying about him, Liam? Your fiancée is not only mad, she's heartbroken. You left her after she told you she was going to have your baby.'

'She told you?'

'Of course. She thought I might have some answers about why you left. I didn't,' she told him. 'But I'm still here looking for you, letting you mess me around with your phony meet-up times, because family is supposed to show up for one another.'

She was out of breath when she was done. Surprised, too. She hadn't expected all of that to come out of her mouth. She knew it was there, but it had always been there. What was different now, that she'd finally said it?

'So you're mad, too.'

'It doesn't matter,' Piper said, fighting for control. 'You need to get your head right with your priorities, man. You're about to become a father.'

'I know,' he said. 'I know. I… I'm scared, Pie. Dad was a terrible father. What if I am, too? I'm already a terrible brother. I'm a terrible fiancé. If the pattern continues, I'll end up being a terrible father.'

Piper exhaled. She knew she should comfort him. Reassure him. But she couldn't do either. Her mind spun around his admission that he'd been a bad brother. That he *knew*. It was the first time he'd ever acknowledged it. She wasn't sure what to do with it.

It inspired her to ask, 'What are you going to do about it, Liam?'

'What do you mean?'

'You have a choice. You choose who you want to be. You don't have to be terrible if you don't want to be.'

'Easy for you to say.'

'No,' she said quietly. 'It's not. It's hard, actually.' She took a breath, hoping the air would settle her. 'Brad was like Dad, Liam. I didn't know it until it was too late. By then, the damage was already done.'

'Pie.'

It was all Liam said, his voice strained. It was oddly comforting.

'I managed to break up with him, and I vowed never to let anyone treat me that way again.' Her heart thudded, her mind stirring. She didn't pay attention to why. 'I chose not to let the past repeat itself. You can, too. If Emma is at all important to you, if your unborn child is, you *should*.'

He didn't respond immediately.

'Tomorrow. Same arrangements as today. I promise I'll be there.' He paused. 'Come alone, Pie. We need to talk.'

CHAPTER THIRTEEN

'WE MEET TOMORROW. Same time and place as he wanted to meet today.'

That was all Piper said when she returned to the restaurant. Caleb hadn't been able to follow her—their plates were full, and he still needed to pay. He'd weighed it up, figured their conversation couldn't be that long, based on past experience. She'd been gone for about ten minutes; he'd been getting ready to go after her when she finally came back.

And that was all she said.

He waited for her to say more. Through the dinner they finished though it was slightly cold. Through the trip back to the house. But she was silent. When he tried to ask her about it, she was reticent.

She walked straight to her room when they got to the house, not giving him a chance to ask her anything. He let her go. What choice did he have? He'd asked her about it. He'd been straightforward. If she didn't want to tell him, that was her decision. Damn the fact that they'd spent two incredible days together. The night they'd shared didn't seem to matter either. Once again, they were two strangers who didn't share their thoughts and feelings.

He managed to resist for the entirety of his shower. The moment he was in his clothes again, he marched up the stairs.

'What the hell?' she asked when she saw him.

She was standing in the doorway of her bathroom, a towel wrapped around her body. Her magnificent hair was piled on top of her head. Water trickled down from it over her face.

'You're wet,' he said.

'Thanks for pointing that out.'

She gave him a look of disdain before grabbing a bottle from the vanity and going back into the bathroom. She shut the door for good measure.

He deserved it.

He was a complete idiot for storming into her room. She deserved privacy. He had no right to be in her space without asking. He left her to it, disgust at himself taking him to the kitchen. He poured himself a shot of whisky, hissing at the burn of it in his throat. Then he went outside, back to the deck where she'd come to him the night before. She found him there again twenty minutes later.

'That wasn't—'

'I'm sorry,' he interrupted. 'I know what you're

going to say. I shouldn't have come up there and I'm sorry.'

She searched his face. 'As long as you know you were crossing a line.'

'I'm apologising for it.'

'You are.'

She angled her head in what he assumed was acceptance of his apology. Then she sat down on the lounger opposite his. She took the long plait she'd braided her hair into and rested it over her shoulder.

'Liam wants me to see him alone tomorrow.' Her eyes met his. 'I think I should.'

He yanked the *no* from the tip of his tongue, knowing he'd stop the conversation before it even started if he said it. He resisted the urge to curl his hands into fists. Refused to sit on them either when that seemed like less effort. The strain of controlling himself so precisely made his heart thud. He thought it would be worth it if he could have a conversation with Piper where he'd convince her not to go alone to see her brother.

'Why?'

It was the only word the control would allow him to say.

'He…he's scared,' she said slowly. 'I think he wants to talk with me about our family issues.' She lifted a shoulder. 'He needs this.'

'Him or you?'

She blinked. 'Excuse me?'

'Does he need to talk about the family issues, or do you?'

'I'm not sure how you came to that conclusion,' she said, her brow furrowing. 'I have no horse in this race. He's the one who ran away from his wedding.'

'You have no horse in this race,' he repeated. 'So shutting me out earlier had nothing to do with you worrying about what's happening between us?'

He wasn't offended by the surprise in Piper's eyes. How could he be when the question came from nowhere for him, too? His control had apparently snapped and words were hurtling out unchecked. Now that they were in the open, Caleb had no choice but to realise that his anger had flared again when Piper hadn't opened up to him about that phone call. It wasn't logical, and it told him that he was worrying about what was happening between them, too.

All the *we have this moment* stuff he'd been telling himself over the last day had been hiding the fact that he was scared. He didn't like the feeling. It reminded him too much of how he'd been after his father died. Terrified of letting his family down. Of letting his father down.

Was that what was happening here, too? Was he scared of what would happen with his siblings once he got back to Mykonos? Was he scared of letting them down? Was he scared of letting Piper down?

'I think,' Piper said, standing up, 'that we should save this conversation for when our emotions aren't so close to the surface.'

'You mean, when you're not this scared?' he asked recklessly. Hell, the control was already gone. He might as well lean in.

Her eyes went cool. 'Goodnight, Caleb.'

'No, Piper, please,' he said, standing. 'I'm sorry. I shouldn't have—' He broke off when he realised he would be lying if he said he shouldn't have said that. 'I need to know.'

'Why?'

'Because something's happening here. I need to know I'm not the only one freaked out about it.'

There was a flicker of emotion on her face before it cleared. He didn't know what she was thinking or feeling. It was torture.

'You're not,' she said when the silence stretched so long he thought she wouldn't answer. Then she turned on her heel and left him with his thoughts.

He watched her leave before he went back to his room. He closed the doors and the blinds. It was utterly dark, the only light coming from the moon shining through the window high above the doors. His housekeeper had replaced the sheets, so he wasn't sure why, when he lay on the bed, he could still smell Piper.

He left the air-conditioning off, turned the fan

on instead. Then he lay and watched it spin. His eyes adjusted, his body sank into the bed. It didn't help him fall asleep. His thoughts were a mess of regret and guilt from the past and the present. In some illogical twist of time, he thought it came from the future, too.

This moment felt significant. As if his actions now would affect the rest of his life. His happiness. No wonder he couldn't sleep.

The tension between her and Caleb was her fault. She knew it and, despite the fact that she longed for things to be different—she wanted to go back to Piper and Caleb on the beach, in the ocean, at dinner, in his room—it couldn't be. At least not until she saw her brother.

'I was thinking about it last night,' Caleb said during breakfast.

Piper had woken up to hear his housekeeper in the kitchen, cooking. Though she would have liked to cook breakfast herself, that urge was overwhelmed by the relief that she didn't have to be alone with Caleb.

'Yes?'

'You should see Liam alone. But I'd like to take you, and wait nearby in case you need me.'

She wanted to protest. Looked into his eyes, saw the desperation and the defiance there. This was the best he was willing to offer. She didn't have the energy to argue. She gave herself a moment to think about whether that was because of her tendency to let people control things, or because she was picking her battles. Was she being naïve, or was she being smart?

She'd lost her ability to discern between the two at some point during her time with Caleb. She'd gone from doubting everything he said to doubting nothing. She'd told him she was terrified the night before, and this was why. Because she didn't know if she was losing herself as she lost her heart to him.

Oh, no. She was losing her heart to him.

'That's fine,' she said in a thin voice. 'You'll need to give us some space, but that's fine.'

'You won't see me, I promise.'

The politeness they were treating one another with would have bothered her more if she weren't so concerned by the revelation that she was falling for him. Of course she had known. On some level. Otherwise the fact that she'd told her brother she was choosing a different life wouldn't have bothered her so much.

But here now, actually admitting it to herself? It sent wave after wave of panic through her. She could barely finish the fruit bowl she'd made herself. She didn't touch the croissant she'd put on her plate as an afterthought to have with her coffee. Her stomach was tightening, her heart pulsating heavily against her chest. All because she was starting to feel something for Caleb—and because she knew who she was.

The same Piper. Beneath her progress and her determination to choose a different life, there was the same old Piper. That Piper would talk herself into believing that Caleb's controlling tendencies wouldn't affect her. She understood them now and couldn't judge him for it, but that didn't mean she wouldn't find herself back to where she'd been with Brad. Or did it? She didn't know. And that uncertainty was why she couldn't fall for this man.

She excused herself from the table, not bothering to give Caleb an explanation. In her room, she packed up her things. Things he'd bought her, for heaven's sake! She pushed at the thought— she'd pay him back, even if it meant not making rent for a month—and went downstairs. He was standing at the foot of the staircase.

'You want to leave after meeting Liam?' he said, taking one look from her bag to her face.

'Yes.'

He nodded. Shoved his hands into his pockets. 'Okay. Should we buy tickets online?'

'We?'

'Yeah,' he said. 'Regardless of whether Liam pitches, I've been away from Emma too long. She needs me. And it isn't fair of me to expect Tate and Jada to take all the responsibility for the guests.'

All the aching inside her stopped for a moment. She looked at him, at the sincerity of his expression, and couldn't be upset that the warning signs of her body had taken a break. The care this man had for his family was admirable. It was part of why she liked him so much.

The judgement she'd had for her feelings eased. Because when she looked at him like this, when she heard his concerns about his siblings, she could almost imagine she wouldn't lose herself with him.

'Of course,' she said when the moment caught up with her. 'We can do it right now.'

They bought the tickets, packed up and left the house much earlier than they needed to. But what were they going to do there? Lounge around the pool, ignoring one another? Take a swim, not speaking? It was torture not being friends. Well, not friends, since she didn't think that was what they were, but *friendly*. Especially when she knew what it was like.

When they reached the place she was supposed to meet Liam, it was an hour too early. They got out of the car, then stared at one another.

'What do you want to do?' he asked.

'I'm not sure.' She looked around, saw only buses and shops. Then a man in a red shirt passed them, a crowd following behind him. Piper looked at Caleb. 'What do you think they're doing?'

'A tour, probably.'

'A walking tour?'

'I assume.'

Piper narrowed her eyes as she stared after the crowd.

'Twenty minutes. We walk with them for twenty minutes and then we come back. It'll give us twenty minutes to spare before Liam gets here.'

'Are you sure?' he asked mildly.

'Yes.'

Anything to escape the tension.

She didn't wait to see if he was following her; she knew he would be. Soon they were walking along a narrow path surrounded by white buildings. They stopped in front of a whitewashed church, where she and Caleb hung back far enough from the group that the guide didn't notice them. They got some of the history, but Piper was more interested in the architecture. The church had a blue dome on top of it, a signature of Santorini architecture, and a bell beneath the roof.

The group began walking again, but they didn't follow, since the guide had said their next stop would be in twenty minutes.

'We should have done this yesterday,' she told him with a sigh. 'I would have loved to see the wine estate they're going to next.'

'I'm sorry.'

She waved a hand. 'It isn't your fault. I suggested the beach.'

There was a beat. 'I don't regret yesterday.'

She turned at the emotion in his voice. Caught her breath at the emotion on his face.

'Most of it, anyway,' he said with a small smile. 'Should we get going?'

'I don't regret it either,' she replied, ignoring his question. 'I didn't mean it in a "I wish we could go back and replace the day with something else" kind of way. Or with someone else.'

'I wish I could go back and change whatever happened that made things so awkward between us.'

'Would you like to change me?' she asked playfully, desperate not to think about the way her heart cracked at his question.

'Never.' He took a step closer. Cupped her face. 'I wouldn't change you for the world, Piper. You're perfect the way you are.'

He lowered his head, but not enough for their lips to touch. He did so purposely, she knew. Wondered why the action had the judgement of her feelings for him going down another notch.

But she didn't spend much time dwelling on it. Instead, she closed the distance between them, moaning when the contact banished the doubt inside her. When it was replaced with a certainty that this was supposed to be happening. This kiss had an urgency that none of the others had. Even when they'd been deep in exploring one another the other night, it hadn't felt like this. Desperation spurred the movement of their tongues. Passion directed their hands.

Vaguely Piper thought about the fact that they were in public. Less vague was the thought that no one was around. The walking tour group had left a while ago. Caleb had her against the wall, angling her so that they were obscured from the main path.

She let herself sink into it. The urgency, the desperation, the passion. She loved the taste of him. Mint and the faintest hint of coffee. Her hands memorised the shape of him. The ripples of his abs, the curves of his chest, his biceps. Her head dropped back when he moved his lips from her mouth to her neck. Moaned when his tongue brushed over the sensitive skin in the nape of her neck, when his teeth gently nibbled on her. Pleasure meshed with pain and she gasped, putting a hand on her chest in protest.

In thanks.

He pulled away, his chest heaving, his eyes glazed with pleasure.

'I...got carried away.'

She scraped her nails down his chest, over his abdomen. 'We both did.'

He took a breath. 'You're dangerous.'

'So are you.'

His mouth lowered to take hers again, softer this time. She melted against him, marvelling at his skill, his intuition. She didn't care that those things must have come from practice. She only cared that he was using them on her. Making heat pool in the pit of her stomach. Making her ache with a longing she'd never felt. Didn't think she'd wanted to until now.

When he pulled away from her he smiled, brushed her hair back. Tentatively placed a kiss on her lips. Then he looked her directly in the eyes.

'I'm scared, Piper. Terrified.' He tilted her chin with his fingers. 'You're not alone.'

CHAPTER FOURTEEN

PIPER ONLY REALISED she'd been holding her breath when Liam walked into the restaurant and the air gushed from her lungs. It took her a moment to find it again, as if her lungs had forgotten how to function. Once she reminded them by going through the motions of breathing carefully, she raised a hand and got his attention.

The first thing she thought was that he looked terrible. There were bags under his eyes, his skin looked ragged, and he walked as if the world was on his shoulders. The second thing she thought was that he needed help. So when he reached the table she stood and pulled him into a hug.

His body was stiff at first, then slowly he relaxed and folded his arms around her. They stood like that for longer than they had hugged before—though this wasn't a feat. They hadn't really hugged before. The only memories she had were before he'd left for university, and after their father had died. When they'd realised they were finally free.

She stepped back, patted him awkwardly on the shoulder, and they sat. She waited for him to speak.

'Thank you for coming,' he said eventually. He took the glass of what she'd ordered, drank as if he'd come from the desert. 'I know you didn't have to.'

'I did,' she said. 'Not only because your fiancée asked me to, but because you're my brother.' She let it sit. 'But the first might not matter any more if you have no intention of marrying Emma.'

He gaped at her. 'What? Of course I'm still going to marry Emma.'

'You should probably let her know that, then.'

'She doesn't?'

'You ran away the night she told you she was carrying your baby. What do you think she's thinking right now?'

'Good riddance,' he said bitterly.

Piper sighed. 'You need to get over this, Liam.'

'Over what?'

'Your self-pity.' She didn't mince her words. Had neither the patience nor compassion to do so. She did have empathy though, which meant that she knew what her brother needed. Tough love. 'You've made this all about you. You feel sorry for yourself.'

'It is about me.'

'Oh, are *you* pregnant?' she asked. 'Carrying a baby, are you? It's wreaking havoc on your body and your emotions and your fiancée's just left you after you told her you're expecting?'

There was a silence before he mumbled, 'You're supposed to be on my side.'

'There is no "supposed to" when it comes to us, Liam,' she said, careful when his words hit a nerve. 'We were supposed to be a family with Dad. You were supposed to be my big brother.' She waited a beat. 'No one in their right mind would have called you, me and Dad a family. And big brothers… Well, they're not supposed to leave their baby sisters to fend for themselves against controlling fathers.'

He blanched at that. She didn't try to make him feel better. Didn't try to make herself feel better either. She accepted the pain of it, let it wash over her so that one day she'd know when it washed through her.

At some point during the silence Liam's entire demeanour changed. He straightened his spine, drew his shoulders back. He pushed the wild curls of his hair back—they shared at least that familial connection—and looked her straight in the eyes.

'You're right.'

She was holding her breath again. It took those two words for her to realise it, but they were enough. Again, she found herself focusing on her breathing. Then he was talking and she forgot to focus on anything besides his words.

'I wasn't there for you. I should have been.'

She swallowed. 'Thank you.'

'Don't thank me, Pie,' he said with a humour-less smile. 'You have every right to be angry with me. Just like Emma does.' His voice dropped at that, his brow lowering. He shook his head. 'I was a bad brother. I'd... I'd like to change that.'

Her heart swelled. When Liam reached out to cover her hand with his, it burst. She gasped in air, then realised her breathing had turned shallow and took a deep breath, then another. Liam didn't look amused or concerned. He only waited for her. She gave him the go-ahead with a slight nod.

'I couldn't stop thinking about what you said last night about choosing to be better.' He ran a hand over his face. 'I got in here a few minutes ago and I still didn't know why... I was still whin-ing.' He gave her an embarrassed smile. 'I blamed the world for what Dad did to us. Asked *Why me?* too many times to count.'

'I did, too,' she said softly. 'Especially after the whole thing with Brad. I couldn't believe I'd gone down that path. That I'd chosen it. I blamed—' She broke off before she could say *myself.* Not because it wasn't true. Because she didn't want to admit it out loud. 'The world,' she finished lamely. 'I blamed the world, too.'

Liam squeezed her hand, then folded his arms. 'You know, I never liked Brad.'

'What?' she said, dropping her head. When he

smiled at her, she laughed a little. 'Would have been nice of you to tell me that sooner.'

'Would have,' he agreed. 'I should have stepped in. Not to tell you what to do, but to warn you so you could make the decision for yourself.' He exhaled. 'We're a mess, kid. Now I'm supposed to be a husband and a father as a mess.'

'Do you love her?'

'More than anything else.'

'Then you'll clean up. You'll step up.' She nodded at him. 'One, because she'll force you to. Emma's not going to allow you to be anything less than a good dad and husband.'

'I have her brother to thank for that.'

'Why?' she asked, curious despite the warning bells in her brain.

'She's never had to compromise on anything. She always had a good role model in him.' Liam blushed. 'I've always felt like I have to measure up.'

'You do,' Piper said. 'She deserves someone who loves and treats her like Caleb does. You have to do better. And you will.'

His lips curved. 'Was that the second thing?'

'What do you mean?'

'You said "one" when you told me I'd step up. What's two?'

'Oh.' She leaned forward. 'Two, you'll stop running.'

Panic fluttered over his face. 'I don't want to

run. I just… I worry that I'm going to let her down like I let you down.'

'You only let me down because you ran, Liam.' She let the realisation move around in her mind. 'It was kind of okay, what Dad did to us, because we were together. It wasn't that he was doing it to me, it was that he was doing it to us, and that seemed less personal.' She took a breath. 'When you left…'

'It was like he was doing it to you.'

'Yes.'

He reached over, linked their hands. 'I'm sorry, Piper. I should have come back. I didn't because—'

'I know why you didn't,' she interrupted, thinking about all the times she'd wished she could run away. When she'd had the opportunity to leave, she hadn't come back either. Until her father had died, she hadn't gone back to that house.

What would she have done if she'd left a sibling behind?

She almost laughed out loud when she realised she wouldn't have done what Liam had done. Her presence in this small Greek café proved that. Liam hadn't done anything to earn her loyalty, and yet she was there, trying to help him. There was no way she would have done what he did. Hell, she was more likely to have sacrificed her own life, like Caleb had, than do what Liam had done.

But she understood the impulse. Understood that someone who had different priorities might not have come back. Liam hadn't.

It made her like Caleb even more, which was a problem with the way things currently were between them.

She exhaled. 'It's not about what you did, Liam. It's about what you'll do.' She paused. 'What are you going to do?'

The panic that had been on his face was replaced with determination. 'I'm going to stop running.'

'You let him leave?' Caleb asked, indignant. He looked at the café behind Piper, hoping to spot Liam. Hoping that what she'd told him wasn't true.

'He'll be at the wedding,' she assured him.

'And I'm supposed to believe that?'

'That's what he said. I believe him.'

'Why?' he asked. 'He's done plenty of things that mean he won't keep his word.'

'He also pitched up today.' She was being infuriatingly calm. Unmoved. As if the entire wedding didn't depend on a man who had already proven he was unreliable. 'He'll do it again.'

'That's naïve,' he said through clenched teeth. 'Especially after everything he did to you.'

Her eyes went cool, his only warning that he'd overstepped the mark.

'I didn't tell you about my past so that you can throw it in my face. Especially when, when we started this, *you* were using my relationship to him as a reason I should go with you.'

'That was Emma's idea. Besides, I didn't know about what he did then.' He sighed. 'I'm sorry. I'm a bit…stressed.'

'I can see that,' she said dryly. 'Let me guess— you spoke to one of your family members while you were waiting for us.'

'Emma. She's not doing well.'

'That's understandable.'

'I wanted to give her good news when we got back.'

'Again, understandable.'

'You also understand then why you telling me you let him go to do whatever the hell he wants to frustrates me.'

'Caleb,' she said, again in that irritatingly calm voice, 'this isn't your responsibility.'

He gritted his teeth. 'So you don't understand.'

She studied him, looked at her watch. 'We've got to get down to the port. Our boat leaves in ninety minutes.'

The gritting became grinding. He couldn't stop it when it was clear she would no longer entertain his questions.

'I can't go without him,' Caleb said when they reached the car.

'Then you're going to miss the wedding, Caleb.'

She paused. 'Liam will be there. And if he's not, the only thing you can do for Emma is support her. It won't be your fault that he doesn't show up.'

'Why are you being so…so—'

'Reasonable?' she asked with a quirk of her brow. 'Because I'm removing my emotion from the situation.'

'It's that easy for you?'

'No, but it's necessary for my sanity.' She put a hand on the roof of the car. 'Does this mean I have to call for a cab, or are you going with me?'

He took a long time to make the decision. When he started driving he was surprised his teeth hadn't become ash, the way he was working them. He forced himself to stop, which allowed him to feel how uncomfortably his heart was beating. As if he had something important to do but didn't know what.

It *was* uncomfortable. The feeling, and the fact that he always knew what to do. Doing nothing wasn't an option. It was never an option. Damn it. He should be looking for Liam. He should hire a private detective. Maybe he could—

A warm hand on his thigh stopped his thoughts. He looked down, felt the warmth spread, then looked up and thanked the heavens nothing unexpected had happened or he might have caused the car to crash.

'Was that really worth your life?' he muttered, taking the turn that would lead them to the port.

'It stopped the downward spiral of your thoughts, didn't it?' she asked, unperturbed.

He didn't answer immediately.

'This is a departure from your initial thoughts on my driving.'

'I suppose I've learnt to trust you.'

The simple sentence became more meaningful with the squeeze of her hand. He opened his mouth. Shut it when he realised he didn't know what to say. Part of him wanted to ask her why she was pulling away from him. If she trusted him, why was she curling into herself, away from him and what they'd shared?

Another part of him thought it was for the best. There was no future for them once they reached Mykonos. That hadn't changed since the last time he'd thought it. And it was a good thing. With the mess he was anticipating with the wedding, Emma would need him more than ever. Then there'd be a baby, and he'd have to help with that. It would be what his father would have done. It was what he wanted to do.

Except he wasn't sure of that any more. He didn't know if he wanted to keep trying to be like his father. He didn't know *what* he wanted. In taking responsibility for his siblings, he'd lost the ability to discern what *he* wanted. It had taken wanting something so badly, and being torn between his family and that thing, for him to realise it.

He was distracted from his thoughts when Piper pulled her hand away and he felt as if he'd lost a limb. It reaffirmed that her pulling away was for the best. In fact, he probably should have done it first. He shouldn't be kissing her in front of churches. Shouldn't be telling her he was scared of falling for her.

Because you already have.

He grunted at the inner voice.

'What?' she asked, looking at him as they boarded the ferry.

'I didn't say anything.'

'You grunted.'

'That's not speaking.'

She sighed, as if he were an elderly person who required patience. Or simply someone who'd admitted to having feelings for a woman when he couldn't afford to. Either worked.

CHAPTER FIFTEEN

HE FELT CURIOUSLY numb when they arrived in
Mykonos. An overload of emotion and realisations had put him in a mood he barely recognised
in himself. It probably explained his reaction
when Jada stormed to his side the moment they
reached the villa.

'Done playing Romeo now, have you?'

'Is that really what you think I've been
doing these last few days?' he asked. '"Playing
Romeo"?'

Jada blinked. 'Well, you've been gone and—'

'I've been looking for Liam, Jada.' His tone
sounded…passionate, though for the life of him
he couldn't figure out where it was coming from.
'I've been spending my time trying to fix things
for one of you, as I tend to do. The least *you* can
do is acknowledge that, and not pretend like I'd
abandoned you to romance Piper.'

He had, of course, been romancing Piper, but
that wasn't why they'd been away. Besides, he'd
realised he'd have to be firmer if he wanted his

siblings not to need him as much. He didn't know how to reconcile that desire with living up to his father's legacy. Perhaps that helplessness was where the passion had come from.

When he looked at Piper and saw pride in her eyes, pleasure rushed into his system. He wondered if that had contributed to the passion, too...

'I'm sorry,' Jada said sincerely. It didn't hide the confusion but, since that was warranted, Caleb didn't doubt she meant the apology. 'It's just that... The guests are suspicious. They haven't seen Emma or Liam in the last two days, nor you and Piper. They're wondering whether something's going on.'

'Have you seen Emma?'

'Of course. *I* know this last-minute trip thing with Liam isn't real.' Jada bit her nails, a clear sign of her stress levels. 'But we told her she needs to stay in her room.'

'She was okay with that?'

'She doesn't exactly want to be around people, so yeah.'

'So you handled it.' Pride and satisfaction mingled inside him, soothing some of his earlier uncertainty about how ready his siblings were for independence. 'Where are the guests now?'

'Beginning Day One of the Countdown party.' When he only dropped his head in question, Jada sighed. 'They're getting ready to leave for the sunset cruise.'

'That buys us some time.'

'But does not help to lull suspicions. Tate's with them,' Jada said. 'He begins to dance every time someone asks him about Emma or Liam or you two.' Her face turned pleading. 'It's been terrible.'

He tried not to laugh at Jada's expression. Or at the idea that Tate was dancing his way through awkward questions. His brother was a terrible dancer, the only one in the family who hadn't inherited that gene. Only Jada had the courage to tell him that though. Since she made fun of almost everything he did, Tate hadn't taken her seriously. Caleb wondered if he'd done something wrong by not being truthful. Then he pictured his brother dancing again and chuckled. Wrong, maybe. Entertaining though.

Thinking about all of it broke the tension he was feeling.

'This isn't funny.'

He sobered. 'No, it's not.' Cleared his throat. 'Okay, the cruise starts with drinks, doesn't it? On the beach.'

Jada nodded. 'That's why I could be here to talk to you.'

'To complain to me.'

'Yes.'

He smiled. 'When do they leave?'

'Twenty minutes.'

He wanted to ask Jada what she thought they should do next. It was a test, he could admit, to see if she could handle things again. But her expression was pleading and, since he hadn't done much while he was away, he gave in.

Surprise, surprise.

He turned to Piper, ignoring the taunting inner voice. 'How do you feel about going back on a boat?'

Her face paled slightly, but she nodded. 'Sure.'

'You're feeling sick?'

'No, I'm fine.' She straightened her shoulders.

'It would be easier for all of us if he just came back.'

'He is,' Piper said, shifting so she could see Jada better. 'He's coming back.'

Jada brightened. 'He is?' She must have remembered she was upset with him because she immediately scowled. 'When?'

'I'm not sure.'

'You're not sure?' Caleb said. 'He didn't tell you?'

'He said before the wedding.' She turned to Jada. 'He'll be back, and if that means I have to get back on the boat to help with the guests' perceptions, that's what I'll do.'

Caleb took a deep breath. Another when he wanted to ask her how the hell she'd let Liam go without an exact time of when he'd be back.

'Jada, go with Piper. Em and I'll be down before the boat leaves.'

'You *and* Em?'

'Yeah,' he said. 'We'll pretend like she's back early, but she shouldn't be alone any longer.'

He walked away before either of them could reply. Got his emotions under control before he knocked on Emma's door.

There was no reply. He knocked again. Heard nothing again. There could have been a million reasons for that. She could be in the shower. Sleeping. She could have her earphones in, listening to music. Another time, he knew he'd give these options more than a cursory thought. Now, though, worry overtook logic. He had flashbacks to that time Emma had decided to drink an entire bottle of wine and he'd discovered her passed out near a puddle of her own puke.

He knew that wasn't a concern now—Emma would never put herself in danger like that again, or her baby—but he didn't know what else to do. He knocked again, called out, got nothing. So he kicked the door open.

The first thing he saw was the mess. The bed was unmade, blankets on the floor, clothes all over the place. The second thing was the open door to the small courtyard, which each of the rooms had. He was there in two seconds and as soon as he got there he turned around, regret reverberating in every part of his mind.

He shook his head—shook it again—then walked out of the door before realising he'd kicked it open and couldn't close it. Before he realised someone else could walk in and see what he'd just seen. Nausea rolled in his stomach. At the fact that he had seen what he'd seen and also at the prospect of seeing it again.

He took his phone out, messaged Jada and waited for her to arrive. He was effectively standing guard at the door. Jada would never let him live this down, but rather her than him. Rather *anyone* than him.

He didn't even blink when Piper arrived instead. To her credit, after she took everything in, she didn't comment.

'I believe you need reinforcements?'

He nodded.

'Why?'

He tilted his head back, towards what he'd left behind.

'I'm sorry,' she said pleasantly. 'I don't understand your non-verbal communication at the moment.'

He glowered at her. She smiled.

'Why do you need reinforcements, Caleb?'

'Emma.'

It was all he could manage. When she peered around him at the open door, he saw alarm in her eyes.

'Is she okay?'

'Fine.'

She narrowed her eyes. 'What's going on, Caleb?'

'Your brother.'

She lowered her head. Made a gesture for him to continue.

'He's in there, too.'

'Liam's in there?' She looked around him again. Obviously, she couldn't see anything. 'Is that why the door's broken? Because you saw him?' She exhaled irritably. 'Boundaries, Caleb. This is ridiculous. They're engaged, and if they—'

'I walked in on them…' He couldn't say it.

'You walked in— Oh. Oh,' she said again, scrunching her nose. 'Oh,' she said for the third time, her face comically arranged. He couldn't find the humour in it yet though.

'I don't think I'll ever…' He shook his head. 'I saw…'

Her eyes widened. Her lips pursed.

He narrowed his eyes. 'It's not funny.'

'Oh, no.'

'Seriously.'

She pressed her lips together so hard they turned white.

'Piper,' he rasped. 'It's not funny.'

A sound burst through her lips. She put a hand over her mouth.

'You don't get it. They're—'

She interrupted him by putting her free hand out.

'Please, don't.' She said it with a little gasp, as

if she'd been holding her breath. 'I don't want to be traumatised.'

'Yes,' he exclaimed. 'That's it. I'm traumatised. I saw my baby sister—'

This time she stopped him by putting her hand over his mouth. 'I said *don't*. I get it. I really do.'

'Then why are you—?' He stopped when she pulled her hand away so he could speak clearly. Started again. 'Then why are you laughing?'

'I'm not. I didn't.' She fluttered her lashes at him innocently. 'Does this look like I'm laughing?'

There was a moment. One single beat where their eyes met, linked. The light of amusement in her eyes was so bright he was caught in it. In her. As if she were the sun and that amusement, that happiness that she still somehow had inside, despite everything she'd been through, were rays heating his cold heart.

In that moment, that beat, his breath caught. His world changed. And he realised, quite simply, that he was in love with her.

Rubbish, the logical part of his brain told him. He'd known her for three days. There was no way he could love her. There was no way he'd fallen for her.

A sound escaped her lips. Laughter. The joy of it went right to his soul, defying logic. And then they were laughing together. Laughing and laughing at his expense, at his trauma. It didn't matter since the bubble they'd been in on Santorini had somehow come back. Bigger, more impenetrable than before.

In his mind, he knew that wasn't true. Bubbles, by nature, were meant to burst. They were easily shattered. There was no such thing as an impenetrable bubble. In his heart, he didn't care about any of it. His chest felt oddly full, oddly light at the same time. And he memorised this moment. Knew that he would need the memory of it when the spell he was under faded or the bubble floated away. Because, deep down, he knew it wouldn't burst.

That was what worried him.

Something had changed. She felt it before they started laughing, but the laughter had been rolling around in her chest, her stomach, for too long and demanded attention. But she felt it. Saw it. Knew that her life would never be the same because of it.

When Liam and Emma staggered through the door of their room, faces flushed—from pleasure *and* confusion, she imagined—it finally caught up with her. Rolled around in her like the laughter had been. Except this didn't have the comforting strokes of the laughter. It was tight and fluttery, like a butterfly stuck in a confined space trying to get out.

'What…um…?' Emma said, putting her hands

behind her back when she saw the two of them there. 'What are you doing here? And why is the door broken?' She blinked as she took in the scene. 'Why is the door broken?' she asked again, her voice more concerned. 'Caleb?'

Caleb didn't look at her. He was still looking at Piper. And she was still looking at him. It took all of her strength to look away. She stepped back, as if that small distance would protect her.

'Caleb!'

He finally turned and looked at Emma. 'What?'

Emma frowned, suspicion clear in the creases between her eyes. 'I asked why the door's broken.'

'I was worried about you.'

'You were—' Her eyes widened, suspicion forgotten. 'Did you come inside?'

'No,' Caleb said immediately. Despite the tight feeling in her stomach, Piper's lips twitched.

'But—'

'He didn't see anything, Emma,' Piper offered, schooling her smile. 'Besides, I'm sure there was nothing to see.'

'No,' Liam agreed, though the flush on his face had long since morphed from what he and Emma had been doing into embarrassment. 'We were… talking.'

Piper raised a brow at her brother. His colour deepened.

'Well,' she said, amused. 'If you're done *talking*, your guests are all convinced the wedding is off.' She turned to Caleb now. 'That's why Jada sent me. She's trying to keep up the façade.' The amusement turned to a full-blown smile. 'She's taken to dancing, too.'

'Jada?' Caleb asked, his head dropping. 'My *sister* Jada?'

Piper only looked at him. Looked away when that felt too intimate. *Damn it.* What was it that had changed?

'Yes. Now,' she directed to Emma and Liam, 'you two better pitch up before Tate and Jada scare off all the guests.'

Emma and Liam exchanged a look, then rushed back into the room. Awkwardly, Piper and Caleb stood guard at the door, not speaking. The tension built with each passing second. By the time Liam and Emma emerged, looking fresh in matching outfits, Piper was trying hard not to shift her weight. She'd only managed due to her pride. Thank goodness Caleb caused that emotion to flare inside her.

She wasn't as happy about the rest of what Caleb caused to flare inside her.

Inadvertently, she lifted her hands to her lips, remembering the kiss from that morning. She dropped her hand when she saw him watching her. When there was a glint in his eyes that told her he knew exactly what she'd been remembering.

Damn it.

Emma chattered happily the entire way to the beach, as if her fiancé hadn't left her three days earlier. Liam looked at her adoringly, and Piper could only sigh at the easiness of it. What she wouldn't give to be able to brush off and forgive as easily as Emma seemed to have. Yes, she'd made progress with Liam, but she wouldn't trust him until he proved he'd meant what he'd told her.

Yet you trust Caleb.

The feeling in her stomach tightened even more. She rubbed a hand there, hoping to ease the ache. She'd meant to comfort Caleb when she'd told him she trusted him. His mind had been burning out, she could see, and she'd wanted him to think of something else. But when she'd said the words—words she'd told herself she'd have to guard against after Brad—she'd found them to be true. Which meant she'd fallen for Caleb.

Her feet stumbled. A strong arm caught her before she could fall. She looked at Caleb in surprise. He hadn't always been walking next to her. Had she really been so caught up in her thoughts of him that she hadn't noticed him there? And why did it feel significant that he'd caught her before she could fall?

Piper.

She straightened, thanking him quietly before walking again, catching up with Liam and Emma, who'd been walking in front and hadn't noticed anything. Nothing could come of thoughts like that. Of the hope that joined them. There was only that fear. That dread. That certainty that this wouldn't end well for her. It never did.

When she'd fallen for Brad, she'd lost something of herself. Trust, primarily, in her judgement. What if Caleb wasn't as good a guy as she thought? No, she couldn't let it happen again. She had too little left to lose. One more bad decision might be the end of her, *especially* with him. If she let herself be with Caleb and things went wrong, she might have nothing left.

'Liam.'

Emma's breathy tone was the only reason Piper knew something had happened. She stopped, only then noticing the white stones on the beach. They were shaped in a heart, with Emma and Liam's initials in them. Around the stones were candles, flickering like the promises Liam now seemed to be whispering in Emma's ear.

She walked away when she realised this was a private moment. Went to join the small crowd who hadn't yet departed. It was as much of a mystery that they were still there as the fact that Liam had managed to arrange a grand gesture. She supposed they were linked somehow, and nodded at Tate and Jada when they both gave her a thumbs-up. She and Liam were apparently forgiven for the turmoil of the last three days then.

She shrugged it off, turned and watched the romantic moment with the rest of the crowd. Caleb joined her and she tried not to stiffen.

'I guess this means they're getting married.'

'Guess so,' she murmured.

'Piper—'

'Oh, look,' she said, partly because she didn't want to hear what he said, and partly because she'd been distracted by her brother and Emma.

Liam had picked Emma up and was swinging her around. The sun had started going down behind them, casting a glowing yellow light over the couple. Emma laughed, wild and happy, something Piper didn't think she'd see from the bride after her groom had run away. Liam looked up at his fiancée tenderly.

Piper wished she had her phone with her so she could capture it. So some day she could show it to Liam and Emma's baby and tell the child that this was the moment she'd known their parents would have a happy marriage.

A lump grew in her throat. She sucked her lip in, bit down on it when the lump kept growing. Her eyes were burning, too. Any moment now she would start crying. Piper didn't know how or why watching her brother be happy made her emotional. The threads of it were weaving together in her mind, showing her a picture that made her hate herself.

She turned, hurried back to the villa. They didn't need her on the cruise any more. Emma and Liam were both there, happy, clearly in love and preparing to marry. There was no more need for pretence.

She wouldn't have been able to manage it anyway. She'd barely been able to hide her emotions, for crying out loud. A slight breeze blew over her; her cheeks felt extra cool, telling her the tears she'd been fighting were falling. She started to run, ignoring the sand pouring into her shoes and the rocks digging into her feet. When she got to her room she shut the door, locked it. She made it to her bedroom before the tears turned into sobs.

She knew why she was upset. Because she would never have what Liam and Emma had. Certainly not with the man she wanted to have it with.

CHAPTER SIXTEEN

His tolerance for pointless conversations had thoroughly been tested this evening. Usually, he was quite good at it. The countless hours he'd spent networking after he'd taken over his father's business had taught him how. He knew when to pretend to be interested when he wasn't. He knew how to hide his annoyance at close-mindedness, or his irritation at having to be there at all. They were skills he was proud of. Tonight, he didn't use one of them.

He was beginning to think love wasn't all it was cracked up to be.

That was the only reason he could think had motivated his behaviour. He'd realised he was in love with Piper, and everything he'd known before that had gone to hell. Then, of course, there was how Piper had acted around him. Tense and skittish. As if she were afraid of him. When she'd run from the beach earlier, he'd wanted to go after her. To demand she tell him why she was acting that way. Or to tell him what was wrong. But Tate had cornered him before he could. His brother had wanted him to talk to the captain of the boat cruise, who wasn't as impressed by all the delays as the guests had been.

He'd been torn. For a full minute he'd stared after Piper, ignoring his brother's nudges. When he'd met Tate's eyes and seen his brother's desperation, he'd recognised it as an opportunity to test Tate's independence. So he'd sacrificed his immediate desire to determine whether he'd be able to prioritise himself in the future.

After some grumbling, his brother had succeeded in calming the captain down. It had been as much of a lesson for Caleb as for Tate. With two of his siblings proving more than capable, and a third getting married, Caleb wondered whether he simply wasn't giving his siblings enough credit. Perhaps they weren't giving themselves enough credit either because of it.

'Caleb!'

He turned, saw Emma coming his way. She seemed deliriously happy. If he didn't know that she hadn't been drinking, he might have thought that happiness artificial. But no. That spark on her face, the bright light in her eyes? Natural. From love. His brow furrowed at the difference between her experience of the emotion and his.

Then again, she had just had three days of awfulness because of it...

'What?' she asked when she reached him.

'*You* called me.'

'But you're frowning.'

He relaxed the muscles between his eyebrows. 'Better?'

'Much,' she said with a grin, before tilting her head. 'You're okay, right?'

'Fine.'

'Fine enough to make sure my door's fixed?' Her cheeks flushed, a reminder of what had happened that afternoon that neither of them wanted to speak about.

'Yeah, sure,' he said quickly. 'I think we might have to move you for the night.'

'I can stay in Liam's room.'

'You're getting married tomorrow, Em,' he protested. 'You can't spend tonight with your fiancé.'

'Yeah, well, I'm already pregnant,' she said, putting a fist on her hip. 'It's not like we're waiting or anything. And the worst thing's already happened to me.' Her face tightened. 'I thought I lost him. So there's no chance of more bad luck.'

He didn't think that logic was sound, but it had been a long day. At random moments, his mind had offered him an image of Piper laughing, or teasing him, or looking up at him as if she felt something for him. Sometimes, he swore he could even taste her. Smell her perfume.

No, he wouldn't burst his sister's bubble. Especially since wanting her to be independent meant he needed to stop trying to control her actions.

He wondered what Piper would say about that realisation.

'Fine.'

'You're the best, Caleb!' she said, smacking a kiss on his cheek. 'Take Liam with you and the two of you can move my bags.'

'I can do that by my—'

It was too late. Emma had already flounced off, the tail of her dress blowing in the wind as she made her way to Liam. Seconds later Liam was walking towards Caleb. He didn't pretend to be excited about it.

'You don't have to help me,' Caleb said, walking from the beach where they'd been since the end of the cruise. 'I can move a couple of bags by myself.'

'I've got the keys to my room,' Liam said, dangling them from his fingers. 'Besides, I think she wants us to talk.'

'What is there to talk about?' Caleb said dryly.

The next kilometre went by in silence.

'Look, I'm sorry about what happened these last three days,' Liam said eventually.

Caleb grunted.

'I know it makes me seem like a jerk. You're probably worried about what Emma's got herself into. But I promise you, I'm a good guy. I'll be good to her, too. I just needed a moment.'

'Are you going to need a moment when your kid does something wrong? Or when Emma annoys you into being a better man?' He shoved his hands into his pockets. Rather that than what he wanted to do with his fists. 'What about when something serious happens? She gets sick or you do or your kid. Are you going to need a moment then, too, Liam? Or are you going to be a good guy?'

'The...the last one.'

They'd reached the villa, which was a surprise to Caleb since he was sure they'd started walking seconds ago. Maybe the anger had fuelled him more than he'd realised.

'Really?'

'Yeah, really.' Liam ran a hand over his face, turned towards Caleb. 'I get why you're asking me this. But—'

'Do you, Liam?' Caleb asked, taking a step closer. He was taller than Liam; he was also the brother of the woman Liam loved. Not quite equal ground, but it worked for intimidation. 'Do you know what it's like to step up for the people you care about?'

'I'm here, aren't I?'

'You say that as if it's enough,' Caleb spat. 'Emma's memory of telling you she's pregnant will always be tainted by you running—literally. As will the memories of her wedding. Not to mention the fact that you don't know what being there for someone means.'

'We're working it out.'

'You better,' he growled. 'Because if I find out you treated my sister the way you treated yours—'

'Caleb.'

The quiet voice stopped him. Only then did he realise he was so close to Liam he could poke the man in the chest. That if he tried hard enough, that poke could force Liam into the pool behind them. The temptation was there, but the voice pulled him. As did the disappointment and warning in it.

He took a step back, turning to find Piper. His heart lifted, soared at the sight of her. She wore a sleep shirt. It was nothing like the one she'd worn in Santorini. That one had been cotton with a high neckline and sleeves that covered her shoulders and some of her arms. This one was silk, with thin straps, dipping between the valley of her breasts. She pulled on the jersey he only now noticed around her, over the magnificence of her. For the first time he saw the swelling around her eyes, the slight pink of it.

'Piper,' he said, taking a step forward. 'What's wrong?'

'For one, you threatening my brother.'

He stilled. He'd already forgotten about Liam, if he was being honest. He clenched his hands tighter in his pockets. It upset him that she was defending a man who couldn't bother to do the same for her.

'Can you give us a minute, Liam?' Piper asked, folding her arms now.

'Are you sure?'

Caleb turned, unamused that Liam was feeling protective *now,* when he didn't need to be. Liam didn't look at him, kept his eyes on his sister. Something about the steadiness of his gaze made Caleb respect him more. If he'd been in the mood, he might have even admitted it.

'Yes.'

Caleb turned back at Piper's answer, waited until they were alone before he spoke again.

'Are you okay?'

'Why would you think that was a good idea?' she asked instead of answering him.

'What?'

'All of it. Getting involved with Emma and Liam's business.'

He gave her a look. 'We've been very involved with Emma and Liam's business for the last few days. Why stop now?'

Her eyes cooled. 'Because they don't need our help any more.'

'You don't think they're going to need help again?'

'Sure. That's what family members do, isn't it? Help one another.' She shook her head. 'I don't get you, Caleb. You've spent all your adult life helping them and *now* you have a problem with it?'

'Maybe I'm tired of helping them,' he snapped. 'Maybe if I get involved now, I won't have to get involved in the future. Maybe I can finally live my own life.'

She studied him. 'You're trying to control the situation now so you won't have to in the future?'

'I can hear the judgement in your voice.'

'I'm not judging you. Or maybe I am.' Her arms went around her waist now. 'Look, I get the control thing was a coping mechanism after your dad died. But why do you still need it? And why do you need permission to live your own life?'

He couldn't answer her. Didn't know how to say the words.

'You're afraid of something,' she said into the silence.

'You're one to speak of fear,' he retorted when his heart thudded hard against his chest at how she'd seen through him. 'We both know you're terrified of what's happening between us.'

Her expression opened. It just opened, and he could see every emotion on her face. It hit him in the chest. Guilt burned with shame in his stomach, ravaging everything around it.

'You're right,' she said. 'I am afraid.' She shrugged. 'But at least I know what I'm afraid of.'

'And what's that?'

'This.' Though everything about her—her stance, her expression—screamed vulnerability, her eyes remained steady on his. 'I'm scared you're going to try and control me. I'm scared... I'm scared I'll let you.'

She'd known the moment would come for her to say it. She hadn't expected it to come so soon. Certainly not the night before Liam's wedding, and certainly not that Liam would be the reason for it. But when she'd heard Caleb's threats she couldn't watch any more. Couldn't let him use her as an excuse for what she now saw was ignoring his fears.

Her tears, her emotions in turmoil earlier that evening—minutes ago, really, until she'd heard voices outside and come out to investigate—had prepared her for this moment. They'd prepared her to say this.

It hadn't prepared her for his reaction.

'You think you'll let me control you?' he asked, his expression one of disbelief. 'You really believe that?'

'I have already.'

'When?'

She opened her mouth, ready to list off all the instances. She couldn't remember one. Not because they didn't exist—she knew they did—but because his disbelief was rattling around her head, bouncing off the examples and causing them to ricochet away.

'I'll wait,' he said, jaw clenched.

'You know you've done it.'

'Yes,' he agreed. 'You've also put me in my place every time I have. Hell, you've made me adjust my behaviour.' His brow knitted. 'I think about how to phrase things around you. I don't want you to think I expect you to do anything, so I ask instead of tell. I suggest instead of state. And not only around you.'

'Brad suggested, too,' she said. She couldn't think what else to say.

'Brad?' he repeated. 'Your ex?'

She nodded.

'You're comparing me to the man who told you how to wear your hair?' he asked. 'The man who probably told you what to say and when to say it, too.'

She didn't bother confirming. They both knew it was true.

'You know why I try to control things, Piper. And as soon as you told me how it made you feel, I stopped doing it. I made an effort not to do it. If it came out, it's because it's been a habit of mine for longer than the three days I've known you. It's how I deal with stressful situations, which the last three days have been.'

He rested one hand on his hip, the other on his head. Then he shook his shoulders and shoved both his hands in his pockets again. It seemed to be his stance whenever he didn't know what to do with his hands. That usually happened when he was frustrated. She knew this because it had happened a lot in the last ten minutes.

'You can't really think I'm like him,' he said softly. It broke her heart. Forced her to face the truth.

'No, you're not.'

He nodded. 'Okay.' Nodded again. 'Okay, we can work with that.'

'Can we?' she asked, her voice broken now, too. 'Because it's not really about you. It's about me. And whether I can do this.'

'You know,' he said after a while, 'it took me a long time to face that I wanted a life of my own. I couldn't even say that out loud. Until you.' His face was the picture of sincerity. 'You made me realise that Emma and Jada and Tate are grown-ups. They can do things on their own. But I've enabled them. Shielded them. Now they expect me to be there every time something goes wrong, and I feel like I'm constantly on call.'

'They'd hate knowing that.'

'Yeah.' He looked down, then at her again. 'You helped me to figure all this out, Piper. Why won't you let me help you do the same?'

Her legs suddenly felt unsteady under her, and she went to sit on the bench under the ve-randa. It was more romantic than it should have been considering the serious discussion they were having. Pink flowers crawled over the wooden planks above them, moonlight shone between the gaps, reflecting in the pool in front of them, too.

She didn't speak until Caleb joined her.

'You like me, don't you?'

His eyes flickered. 'Yes.'

'So you're probably giving me more credit than I deserve.'

'I'm not. In fact, most of the time I tend to give people in my life too little credit.'

He didn't continue for a long while, which made her realise something.

'Including yourself?' she asked.

'What? No.'

'Do you believe that the reason Jada and Tate and Emma are capable is because of you?' she asked. He didn't reply. 'You were an amazing example to them. And you were there when they needed you. You've proven yourself. Give yourself credit for that.'

'But what if I haven't proven myself?' He said it so softly she almost didn't hear him.

'What do you mean?' she exclaimed. 'You've spent all your adult years giving them a life most people only dream of.'

'I'm not talking about them,' he said. 'I'm talking about my father.'

CHAPTER SEVENTEEN

PIPER'S HAND CURLED over his as soon as he said the words. He wasn't sure how he felt about it. Was it comfort or pity? Then he saw the expression on her face, the compassion, and realised it was both. When it came from her though, it didn't feel like a bad thing. It wasn't condescending. It was…caring.

'Why?'

'Remember when you said you sometimes wonder what your mom would have thought about your life?'

'I do,' she replied. 'Not so much about my life, but about what my father did to us, and how things might have been different if she'd been alive.' She shifted towards him. 'Did you mean like that?'

He looked down at their linked hands. Delicate, he thought. Her fingers were long and thin and delicate. He couldn't imagine why that was important now, but it felt as if it was.

'You know I was trying to be like my father

since he died. Part of that was because I feel guilty that I had him and they didn't. Another part is that…' He took his time. 'I was a brat when I was a kid. A real brat, Piper,' he said. 'I didn't listen to my father, didn't help at home. Made him worry about me just about every chance I got.'

'So you were being a normal kid.'

'Normal kids don't *try* to upset their fathers. They do what they do because they're stupid and don't know any better. I wasn't like that. It was… deliberate. I was trying to be a brat.'

'You must have had a reason.'

'I didn't,' he said, hating the warmth her understanding spread inside him. 'Maybe I was acting out because he was there and my mother wasn't. Maybe I was trying to figure out what would get him to leave, too.'

'Like your mom.'

'Yeah.'

'So you had reasons.'

'Not good ones,' he said. 'He didn't deserve it. He was a—' He broke off, sucked in a breath. 'He was a good man. A good father. He did his best, and that was more than…'

He pulled his hand from hers, linking it with his own. He didn't deserve to have her care.

'Now you're trying to prove to him that you're a good man, too.'

'Yeah.' He squeezed his fingers so tight his

knuckles turned white. 'Or I'm saying sorry,' he mumbled, 'for being such a brat.'

'He wouldn't have needed you to say you were sorry. He probably knew that you were going through stuff.'

'Doesn't make it any better. Actions are what matter. Mine weren't great.'

She was silent for a moment. 'You don't think he'd be proud of what you've done now? You've sacrificed your life to take care of your family. You took over the family business. You've done more than enough. You don't have to feel guilty for stepping back now and living the rest of your life.'

'No, I do.'

'Why are you making this so hard on yourself, Caleb?'

Anger stirred, hot and irrational.

'Why are you trying to make it so easy? It's not,' he told her before she could answer.

'You're still scared.'

'I'm not scared.'

'Why?' she asked, ignoring his answer. 'You don't have to be. Everything is going to be okay.'

'I'm *not* scared.'

'You don't have to tell me, Caleb, but you have to work it out for yourself.'

That was the problem; he already had. But it was still messing around with his mind. He needed time to sort through it.

'Is that what you're doing?' He stood now, began to pace. 'Figuring things out and using it as an excuse not to date me?'

'No,' she said, watching him from her spot on the bench. 'I've already figured them out. I can't date you because I'll lose myself with you.'

He stopped walking. 'Did you lose some of yourself these days we spent together?' She opened her mouth but nothing came out. He nodded. 'So you know this is all an excuse, then.'

'Both parties need to be in the right space for a relationship to work, Caleb. Neither of us are.'

'Don't use me as an excuse to not take a chance on us,' he said quietly. 'If you don't want to, that's fine. But it isn't because of me.'

'You're making this more difficult than it needs to be.'

Too late for that.

He didn't say it. If he had, she would know that he was already in love with her. It was as difficult as it could get.

Piper didn't get any sleep. She thanked the heavens for the gift of make-up and the fact that she wasn't a bridesmaid. Hopefully no one would notice the bags under her eyes. And no one would ask her questions that would remind her that she'd sat up all night, looking out of the window, Caleb's words floating around in her head.

She wore a simple red dress to the wedding. It

wasn't flashy, and it would likely clash with the shades of blue of the wedding theme, but it was the first item of clothing she'd bought after she'd broken up with Brad. An act of defiance. She'd walked into the first shop she'd seen, gone right for the colour Brad had hated on her and bought the thing she'd liked the most. It brought her a lot of joy. Today, it gave her a confidence she didn't feel. She left her hair curly, for good measure. Though, honestly, she was still trying to figure out whether she liked it.

Too late to worry about that now, she told herself, checking the time as she finished her make-up. She looked...decent. Like someone who was going to a wedding, which was probably a good thing since she was. But there was something different about the person she saw in the mirror. It wasn't the bags under her eyes or the red dress or her hair. It was the fire she saw beneath it all. The...the *strength*.

She blinked, took a step back from her reflection. She had no idea how she thought that might help. Was she trying to distance herself from her thoughts? Of course not. They were in her head. She couldn't run from them. Surprise was obviously an intoxicating emotion. An illogical one. She'd been surprised by the version of herself she'd seen in the mirror, that was all.

But once it simmered down, once it faded, Piper wondered if that strength was a matter of will. Had she hoped she'd see it there and so saw it? Or was it that Caleb's words—his question of whether she'd allow him to control her—were still floating around in her head, tempting her with the picture they'd created of her?

A strong woman. Someone who could take care of herself. Who could move on with life without wondering when the next person would destroy it. She had that power, didn't she? She could take control of her own life and refuse to allow anyone else to make her feel as if she didn't deserve autonomy. Unless she couldn't.

And believing she could when she couldn't would destroy her even more than *knowing* she couldn't.

She took a shaky breath, grabbed her things and closed the door behind her, refusing to look in the mirror while she finished up. A sigh of relief gushed through her lips as she leaned against the door. She closed her eyes, told herself things would go back to normal soon. None of this would matter when she was back in Cape Town, teaching her kids and living her life.

Alone.

It had always been alone, she told that irritating inner voice. When she'd lived with her father, she and her brother had fought for their lives separately. Then Liam had left and she'd kept fighting. After her father had died she'd had to fight in her relationship with Brad. Alone still. She'd lost more than she'd won, but the most important thing was that she'd walked away. She'd been able to walk away. Alone.

So, stupid inner voice, shut up.

When she opened her eyes she found herself staring directly into Caleb's. Her breath tripped over itself as her heart tried to claw its way to him.

'Hi,' he said after a moment.

His hands were in his pockets again. Since his expression was closed, that was the only thing familiar to her. That stance that told her he wasn't as comfortable as his presence there made it seem. She clung to it. Desperately.

'Hello,' she said carefully. 'What are you doing here?'

'Emma asked me to escort you to the beach.'

She quirked her brow. 'Really? That's the excuse you're going with?'

'Not an excuse,' he said, the side of his mouth lifting. 'She didn't want you to be alone.'

Piper tried not to think about how she'd just had a conversation with herself about being alone. About how she was fine with it. Except with Caleb there she didn't feel alone. For once in her life she felt cared about. The fact that Emma had sent him, had thought to send him, had her insides untying from the knot they were in. And the fact that he was looking at her the way he had the first time he'd seen her with her hair curly made her realise exactly why she was wearing it that way.

How was it possible that he could make her feel so incredibly beautiful with the very thing the men before him had used against her?

Because he's different.

It sent her heart into a panic. Or was that thudding in her chest a result of being in Caleb's presence? He looked good. He was wearing tan pants and a white shirt with a blue blazer. It wasn't quite what she'd been expecting, but she couldn't fault it.

'Did Emma pick out this outfit for you?' she asked.

'Yes.' He sighed. 'I'm sorry you have to see me like this.'

It made her laugh. 'Don't be.' The laughter died when she hesitated. Then decided to go for it. 'I think you look good. Handsome.'

He smiled, though it didn't quite reach his eyes. 'Thanks.'

She took a breath—a reprieve from the awkwardness. 'Let's get going.'

She was so beautiful it made him ache. He couldn't stop looking at her. As they walked down to the beach, he kept sneaking glances her way. That red dress wasn't sin on her. It was too respectable, too simple for that. But it made him *want* to sin. It made him hope. For things she'd made clear she didn't want. Things he had, at some point during his sleepless night, told himself it was better not to have.

When the sun had sneaked into the sky, turning the hazy blue into a canvas of light, he'd convinced himself he didn't want them either. Then he'd seen her standing against her door, her eyes closed. Her skin was striking against the boldness of that red dress, her red lips. And the curls she'd left wild around her face, curls she'd been so hesitant about the day before—only then?—set off a longing so deep his heart composed a song for her. Then beat to the insistent rhythm of it.

'Oh.'

The word drew him from his gloomy thoughts. When he saw where they were, he smiled. Turned to her.

'Shall I?'

'Oh,' she said again, looking at the decline in the path. 'No. I can do this by myself. I did it yesterday.'

'You weren't wearing heels yesterday.'

She bit her lip, breaking the red of her lips with the white of her teeth. He desperately wanted to lean forward, to nip them. He took a deep breath instead.

'It's not a problem if you want to do this by yourself,' he said. 'I don't mind offering a hand instead of my arms?'

Her eyes met his, something deep and meaningful crossing them before she said, 'You can carry me. If you want to.'

He didn't answer that. It was a trap. If he said yes, he wanted to, she might hold it against him. Or realise how desperately he wanted to help her. Hold her in his arms.

'May I?' he asked before picking her up at her nod.

He walked down carefully, things somehow tenser between them than the first time they'd done this. When they were on level ground again, he looked at her. Warm brown eyes blinked back at him. Red lips pursed as a blush spread over her cheeks.

'What?' she asked.

'One dance,' he said. This couldn't be the last time he had her in his arms. He wanted one more time. One he could prepare for and know it was goodbye. 'Give me a dance later and I'll do everything in my power to pretend that nothing happened between us for the rest of Liam and Emma's lives together.'

Her hands tightened around his neck before she relaxed.

'One dance at the end of the night,' she agreed. 'Now, put me down. We have a wedding to attend.'

CHAPTER EIGHTEEN

THE TEARS BEGAN when he saw Emma in her wedding dress.

They'd set up a small area on the beach for her to get ready while the guests got settled a few metres away. He'd thought it all impractical when he'd first arranged it, but seeing her in the small space obscured from the guests with the ocean behind her... Well, the photographer had it right when she said the scene was breathtaking.

'Don't cry,' Emma said when he wiped at the tear that had slid down his cheek.

'I'm not,' he said with a smile. 'It's allergies. Damn sand.'

'You're allergic to sand?' Emma laughed. 'I wish I'd known that before I planned a beach wedding.'

'Like that would have stopped you,' he replied, moving forward to kiss her forehead. He ignored the photographer capturing what he would have liked to be a private moment. He'd already accepted this day would force him to share more with people than he'd like. 'You look beautiful, Em. Liam is a lucky man.'

She smiled at him, bright and cheery like his Em had always been. 'Thanks.' The smile turned into something else. 'But I'm the lucky one, Caleb. I had Dad for eleven years of my life and you for the next thirteen. Good, strong men who loved me more than anything. You helped me to realise what I deserve.' She laughed at Caleb's expression. 'Liam's a good man. He needs to grow up, but he's willing to, you know? He accepts that he needs to change.' She shrugged. 'Besides, I love him. What can I do?'

Pretend love doesn't exist, like I am?

'Anyway, my point is that I was lucky to have you as my big brother.' She cupped his cheek. 'Now I get to move on with my future and forge ahead with life.' She stepped back.

'About that…' He took a deep breath. Prepared to say what he'd told himself he would the night before. 'You probably won't need me as much when you're married.'

Emma frowned. 'What do you mean? Of course I'll need you. You're my brother.'

'And I'll be here for you. As much as I can be.' He cleared his throat. 'But you have Liam now.'

'Yes, I suppose—'

'I think he means Liam should be your first stop, not him,' Jada said from behind him. He had no idea when she'd got there since she'd been outside, checking for the signal from Tate that all the guests had arrived. 'He'll probably be telling me and Tate we need to figure some things out for ourselves next.'

Caleb turned. 'I'm not...' He paused. 'You know how you dealt with all of this stuff while I was away? How you and Tate both did?'

'I know,' she said. 'We can handle things without you. I get it. Got it when you came back from Santorini.'

He nodded. She'd always been the most astute of his siblings. 'I'll still be there for you.'

'I know.' Her lips curved into a sad smile. 'But you deserve some space, too. You've done a lot for us and we...took advantage of it. At least I did.'

'Oh, no,' Emma said softly. 'I think I did, too.'

'Not a great feeling, is it?' Jada asked her.

'I'm not accusing you of anything,' he interrupted. 'I do need some space, but from doing things for you, not from you.' He looked from Emma to Jada. 'You understand that?'

'Of course.' Jada waited a beat. 'I won't even tell Emma what brought on this sudden change of heart.' Her eyes gleamed.

'There's nothing to tell.'

'Really?'

'What are you guys talking about?' Emma asked with a frown.

'Nothing,' Jada said brightly. 'Come on. They were ready ten minutes ago.'

'Ten minutes? Why didn't you tell me? Really, Jada, this is my wedding day and...'

Jada winked at him as Emma ranted, and he realised his youngest sister had distracted Emma on purpose. She mouthed, *I love you.* He smiled, felt warm inside, and wondered how the conversation he'd dreaded had gone more smoothly than he could have hoped.

'Caleb!'

He blinked. 'What?'

'I'm supposed to be getting married.' Emma reached over, grabbed his hand. 'You'll have time to brood later. Right now, you have to walk me down the aisle, big brother.'

If Piper had to describe the event, she would have said it was happy. Emma and Liam laughed their way through the ceremony and their joy spread out to their guests, who realised that the couple shared something special and were grateful to be a part of the moment.

Of course, Piper was, too. Except Emma and Liam's happiness had the opposite effect on her. She brooded on her unhappiness, the fact that she would never be able to celebrate anything like this for herself. It felt cruel. It also felt unnecessary. Was denying herself a relationship, love really the only way she could protect herself? Or was it only baggage from the past? Heavy and slowing her down, keeping her in that place where her ac-

tions were still dictated by the men she'd vowed
never to allow power over her again?

She didn't have answers. Until she did, she was
doing no one any good by staying at the wedding.
She'd done her part. She'd been there, watched her
brother say his vows. She'd had a meal and heard
the speeches. But it was over now. The night was
ending, people were dancing, and Emma and
Liam had already left. There was no more obligation. She could leave.

There's one more obligation.

She ignored the voice, pulling off her shoes
and walking the path to the villa barefoot. She
called the airport, found out there was a plane
leaving in three hours. She threw her clothes into
her bag, called a car and, without another look,
left her room.

'Piper.'

She swore when she saw Caleb there.

'You have to stop doing this,' she told him,
dragging her bag behind her and moving past
him.

'Where are you going?'

'Home.'

'Home?' he asked, tone incredulous. 'Your
flight isn't tonight.'

'Oh, I used all my savings to get myself on a
flight tonight.'

'Why?'

'Because I don't want to be here any more,'

she said. 'I don't want to be around your family and my brother and I definitely don't want to be around you.'

Her bag snagged on a step and she snarled at it when it refused to move, no matter how hard she pulled. Caleb got down, looked at her for permission. She gave it with a curt nod. He gently extricated the wheel from where it had been stuck and the bag came loose easily. It only made her more upset.

'It was nice knowing you, Caleb,' she said, walking to the front of the villa. Damn it, the taxi wasn't there yet. She'd called fifteen minutes ago.

They didn't speak as time passed. She exhaled after five minutes. Gritted her teeth after ten. What was it with her and having to wait for transport?

She aimed a suspicious look at Caleb. 'You aren't my ride to the airport, are you?'

He blinked, then understanding cleared his expression and he laughed. 'No, unfortunately not.'

'Unfortunately?'

His expression turned serious. 'I wouldn't have taken you. Not because I'm trying to control you or anything.' He faced her. 'Because I don't want you to go.'

This was it, he thought, heart hammering. He was making a grand gesture. That was what the movies called it, right? The moment the protagonist proclaimed their love? When his stomach leapt he wondered if it was necessary to do this. Maybe he could simply tell her he wanted her to stay. One look at her expression axed that idea.

'What was the point of that?' she demanded.

'I, er, I want you to stay?'

'Yes, but why would you say that? Obviously I don't want to stay if I'm leaving.'

'Yeah, I get that.' Why was this so hard? 'But I'd like you to stay.' He shoved his hands into his pockets. 'I want my dance.'

She studied him. Ruthlessly, he thought, making him shift his weight from one leg to the other.

'There's a reason I wanted to leave before that dance.'

'What is it?'

'I don't want to be reminded of what we could have.'

He stared. Pulled himself together. 'Why can't we have it?'

'I already told you why.'

'Piper,' he started after a breath, 'I've been... extracting myself from my siblings' lives tonight.'

'What does that mean?'

'I had conversations with all of them about boundaries.' To his surprise—although he wasn't sure why he was still surprised by his siblings— his conversation with Tate had gone as well as the one he'd had with Emma and Jada. 'It proved something I realised recently... I've been living my life for my siblings because it makes me feel closer to my dad. If they're proud of me, maybe he'd be, too.'

Her expression softened. 'Of course he'd be proud of you. I'm sure he is now, wherever he is.'

'Thanks.' He ran a hand over his hair. 'Along with everything else, I've been trying to make up for who I was when he was alive with who I am now. That's why I took charge.'

'I know,' she said with a sigh. 'And there's nothing wrong with that, Caleb. You've done so much for your family and you're a great brother. The best man I know.' She said it with a wry smile.

'Okay,' he said, hope blooming. 'Let's figure this out.'

'No.'

'Piper,' he said flatly, 'I asked my family for space partly so you and I can explore whatever this is.'

'I didn't ask you to do that.' Her expression tightened. 'I told you—it's not about you, Caleb.'

'So there's nothing I can do to change your mind?'

She shook her head, her expression one of torture. 'I'm sorry.'

He told himself to leave it. To set it aside and move on. She'd helped him to the next part of his life. He should thank her for that and go live that next part.

He couldn't.

'You're scared. You're running.'

'I am,' she told him helplessly. 'You know I'm terrified of what I feel for you. It's big and demanding and I'm scared I'll give in to the big demands.'

His heart broke. 'I wish you'd realise how strong you are. How you'd never let that happen.'

'But I have let it happen.'

'In the past. You got through it, and you're even stronger for it.'

The car came then, slowly descending the winding road. Time followed suit, slowing down so much that Caleb held his breath, wondering what her reply would be.

She said nothing.

The car stopped. She handed the driver her bag. When her eyes met his there was an apology there. 'I'll send Liam a message when I'm safe at home.'

And then she was gone.

CHAPTER NINETEEN

IT TOOK HER a month to come to a conclusion.

Some of that could be attributed to her brother and new sister-in-law. They'd knocked on her door ten days after their wedding, honeymoon completed. They did not wear the same happiness as the last time she'd seen them. This time they wore accusation.

'You rejected my brother?'

It was the first thing out of Emma's mouth. With a sigh, Piper stepped back and prepared herself for a conversation that had nothing to do with Liam or his wife. Thankfully, it was short. She first listened to Emma's rant about how her brother had lived for them and the fact that he'd allowed himself to have feelings for Piper was huge. Emma then said that Caleb deserved happiness and maybe Piper wasn't the one to give it to him but she should have at least given it a try.

'Are you done?' Piper asked. Emma nodded. 'Good. One, my business with your brother is private.' She held up her hand at the protest she knew would come from Emma. 'Knowing him, he didn't ask you to come here.' She waited for the affirmation. It came in the form of a nod. 'So there's no reason to get involved. Two—' she pointed at her brother '—why would you think this is a good idea?'

He lifted his hands. 'I'm stuck between a rock and a hard place here.'

'But you're still here.'

He winced. 'To offer support?'

'To whom?' she asked dryly.

Wisely, he didn't answer.

'Look, Emma,' Piper said, voice soft. 'Your brother and I would never work.'

'You mean two people who like and respect one another, who are both level-headed and strong-minded, wouldn't work in a relationship?' Emma narrowed her eyes. 'What are your other excuses?'

None that she'd wanted to share with Emma, considering her mood. Her brother thanked her for that when they left, and Piper thanked him for their concern. It was something, she supposed. A small thing that on the surface felt intrusive, but deep down showed her how her life had changed. Especially since Emma had hugged her afterwards, whispering into her ear that she only wanted them to be happy.

Emma's words stayed with her, as did Caleb's parting words to her. And her life changing? It felt as if it came from the strength both those Martins claimed she had. She had left her father when she'd had enough, same with Brad. Maybe that woman she'd seen in the mirror before the wedding *did* exist. Maybe she needed to trust herself more. Give herself more credit. Not allow her past to affect her any more. She'd made one real mistake—Brad—since her father hadn't been her fault. And was one mistake worth sacrificing a lifetime of unhappiness?

Her answer to that was the reason she'd asked Emma and Liam to help her get into Caleb's house. Why she'd decorated his backyard with flowers and candles and fairy lights. Why she had music playing when he got home. She'd concluded that she deserved to try with Caleb. And that she missed him. And that she *might* be in love with him.

She was definitely attracted to him, she thought when he walked into the yard. He wore a black suit, perfectly tailored, with a green shirt. Her mouth almost watered. Then his eyes rested on her and his eyebrow quirked.

'What are you doing here?'

'I owe you a dance, don't I?'

The next moments were slower than any other in her life. He studied her, then walked towards her, taking her into his arms and gently swaying to the beat.

'It's also payback,' she forced herself to say,

though she wanted to rest her head on his chest and stay there for ever, 'for all those times I walked out of my room in Greece to find you there.'

He laughed softly. 'You're lucky Em and Liam waited outside to warn me someone was here.'

'They told you I was inside?'

'Not in so many words.'

She searched his face. 'You don't look upset.'

'Am I supposed to be?'

'Yes. I would be if you'd left me in Greece and pitched up a month later.'

He angled his head. 'I guess I've learnt to accept that some things are outside of my control.'

'Wow,' she said with a small smile. 'Growth.'

'That wasn't a jab at you,' he said gently. Laughed when she raised her eyebrows. 'Okay, fine, maybe it was, a little. But things have changed since Greece. I've changed.'

'Not too much, I hope.' When his eyes softened, her insides did the same. 'How have the changes been going?'

'I'm not sure.' His brow knitted. 'I have a lot more free time since the kids stopped calling me to fix their problems.'

'You're okay with that?'

'They are, which makes it okay with me.'

'Of course they are.' She squeezed the hand at her waist. 'You made sure of that.'

'I know.' He smiled at her surprise. 'I'm trying.'

She took a breath. 'Me, too.'

'What does that mean?'

'For one, I'm keeping overdue promises,' she said. His lips twitched. 'For another... I don't know. I guess I'm letting myself be okay that I've made mistakes in my past.' She bit her lip. 'I let that control me, too. The fear of what happened repeating itself, I mean.'

'But not any more,' he said softly.

She smiled. 'Not any more.'

It was hard for him to imagine Piper was there for any reason besides reconciliation. He wasn't sure what they were reconciling, for one, since they'd never had a relationship. But pesky things like facts didn't matter to hope. The emotion bloomed so large, so bright inside him that the last month of misery was almost worth it.

He didn't rely on it though. Not until he was sure.

'That morning of the wedding,' she said, speaking marginally louder than the wind that rustled through the trees around them, 'I saw a different woman in the mirror. I think the scales were falling from my eyes. Or I was seeing myself like you did.' She paused. 'Either way, I didn't recognise who that was and it scared me. Until I realised it was a good thing. I didn't see the old Piper. Just this one. Someone who believes in herself. Who wants to, anyway, starting with trusting myself.'

'Piper, that's amazing,' he said, squeezing her hand though what he really wanted to do was kiss her lips. She'd painted them a glorious pink that popped against the white dress she wore. Man, he'd missed looking at her.

'Thank you.' She gave him a shy smile. 'You helped, you know.'

'No,' he denied. 'It was all you.'

'No,' she said with a shake of her head. 'You helped. You forced me to see myself in a different light. To see myself like you see me.' Her eyes sparkled up at him. 'I didn't want to believe it at first. How could I possibly be the strong woman you described? Then I realised I needed you to help me see it. Because you're the right man. And I appreciate you.' She blew out a breath. 'I'm hoping I'll get more opportunities to prove that to you…'

The hope within him turned to her, its sun, opening up like a sunflower. 'What do you mean?'

There was a beat of silence.

'You helped me,' she said slowly, 'because my feelings for you forced me to be honest with myself. To weigh up whether my fears or my love for you was more important.'

'You're…you're in love with me?'

Her face flushed. 'Maybe. Like seventy per cent? We still have a way to go, but I think it'll reach a hundred pretty soon.'

'This is the weirdest love proclamation I've ever heard.'

'Aren't you lucky?'

He laughed, leaned his head on her forehead. 'You're amazing, you know that?'

'I'm getting there.'

'I'm already there,' he informed her. 'You keep me on my toes, Piper.'

'Same here.'

'You're stronger than anyone I know,' he whispered.

'And you're the best man I know,' she whispered back. 'I trust you. With my heart.'

'It'll be my greatest responsibility to take care of it,' he replied, and kissed her.

EPILOGUE

HIS WEDDING BEGAN with a crying woman. Fortunately it wasn't his soon-to-be wife, who, his youngest sister told him, was as calm as a therapist.

It was Jada's comparison, not his. He figured it had something to do with the fact that she was currently doing her postgraduate degree in psychology. He wondered if it wasn't Jada, then, who should be left the task of dealing with Emma's tears.

'You're…getting…married and you've done… so much for…the family…and…and the business and Dad would be…so proud,' Emma said between sobs.

He patted her on the back, made eye contact with his brother-in-law. 'What did you do to her?' he asked.

Liam grimaced. 'I think it's the hormones.'

'You can't keep bringing that up,' he said. 'Lacey's two.'

'Not Lacey.' Liam grinned. 'Baby number two.'

Caleb's eyebrows rose, then he laughed and drew his sister into a hug. 'Champ, you're going to have another one?'

'I know,' she wailed. 'What if I'm not ready?'

He let Liam deal with that when he intervened, drawing Emma out of Caleb's room and letting him enjoy his breakfast in peace. Tate was there, but the youngest of his siblings knew the value of quiet. It was part of the reason he was the best man. When Liam returned—his only grooms-man—he was sans Emma.

'Sorry,' he said. 'We only found out a couple of days ago. She's processing.'

'Near my fiancée?' Caleb asked, worrying about what that energy would do to Piper.

'Yeah, but Piper's beyond relaxed. She managed to calm Emma down and she and Jada are talking about how fun it would be to have another baby in the family.' Liam gave Caleb a suspicious look. 'Something you want to tell me?'

Caleb snorted. 'No.'

Disappointment crushed the suspicion. 'Damn it. For a second there I thought I wouldn't be the only one going through this.'

'There's an easy way to keep from going through this,' Tate commented in his quiet way. Caleb laughed while Liam scowled. It was that kind of easiness that took him to the altar.

He had no nerves as he stood waiting for Piper. More…anticipation. Relief that they'd finally be married. They'd taken it slow for three years, figuring out how they were going to try with one another. When they'd settled into it—when he was no longer worried about proving something to his father; when Piper didn't go quiet every time they disagreed on something—he'd proposed. Yeah, it had taken longer than he'd liked. But they'd worked for their love. Now, their marriage.

The music began to play. Piper appeared at the end of the aisle, and he knew he'd never worked for anything more important.

Later, after they'd said their vows and celebrated—when they were alone in their room, the sliding doors of the Santorini house they'd once stayed in open—Caleb drew Piper close in his arms.

'How did you like your wedding, Mrs Martin?' he asked, kissing her forehead.

She snuggled into him, looked up with a sleepy smile. 'It was the best day of my life. I especially liked your wedding gift.'

'The Piper Martin Dog Shelter?'

'A bit wordy, but I'm sure the dogs won't mind.'

He chuckled. 'To think I signed up for a lifetime of this.'

'You wouldn't want it any other way,' she said, kissing his chest. 'I love you, Mr Martin.'

'One hundred per cent now?' he teased.

She laughed. 'Maybe more. But since I have to keep you on your toes, you'll never know.'

He chuckled again, pressing a kiss into her hair.
'I love you.'

'Good.'

Caleb couldn't have agreed more. It was good.
It was all good.

* * * * *

If you enjoyed this story,
check out these other great reads from
Therese Beharrie

From Heiress to Mom
Second Chance with Her Billionaire
Her Festive Flirtation
Surprise Baby, Second Chance

All available now!